For Nicole

Text copyright © 2022 by Suzanne Lang
Cover art and interior illustrations copyright © 2022 by Max Lang

All rights reserved. Published in the United States by Random House Studio, an imprint of
Random House Children's Books, a division of Penguin Random House LLC, New York.

Random House Studio and the colophon are registered trademarks of Penguin Random House LLC.

RH Graphic with the book design is a trademark of Penguin Random House LLC.

GRUMPY MONKEY is a registered trademark of Pick & Flick Pictures, Inc.

Visit us on the Web! rhcbooks.com

Educators and librarians, for a variety of teaching tools, visit us at RHTeachersLibrarians.com

Library of Congress Cataloging-in-Publication Data
Names: Lang, Suzanne, author. | Lang, Max, 1982- illustrator.
Title: Grumpy monkey who threw that? / by Suzanne Lang ; illustrated by Max Lang.
Description: First edition. | New York : Random House Studio, 2022. |
Audience: Ages 5–8. | Audience: Grades K–3. | Summary: When Jim Panzee is banished from the
jungle after making Oxpecker mad at him, his best friend Norman joins him, but when they end up
in the desert and Norman is miserable, Jim agrees to apologize so they can go back home.
Identifiers: LCCN 2021047969 (print) | LCCN 2021047970 (ebook) |
ISBN 978-0-593-30605-5 (hardcover) | ISBN 978-0-593-30606-2 (library binding) |
ISBN 978-0-593-30607-9 (ebook)
Subjects: CYAC: Chimpanzees—Fiction. | Jungle animals—Fiction. | Mood (Psychology)—Fiction.
| Friendship—Fiction. | LCGFT: Picture books.
Classification: LCC PZ7.1.L3437 Gw 2022 (print) | LCC PZ7.1.L3437 (ebook)
| DDC [E]—dc23

MANUFACTURED IN CHINA
10 9 8 7 6 5 4 3 2 1
First Edition

GRUMPY MONKEY

WHO THREW THAT?

By Suzanne Lang

Illustrated by Max Lang

RANDOM HOUSE STUDIO ⌂ NEW YORK

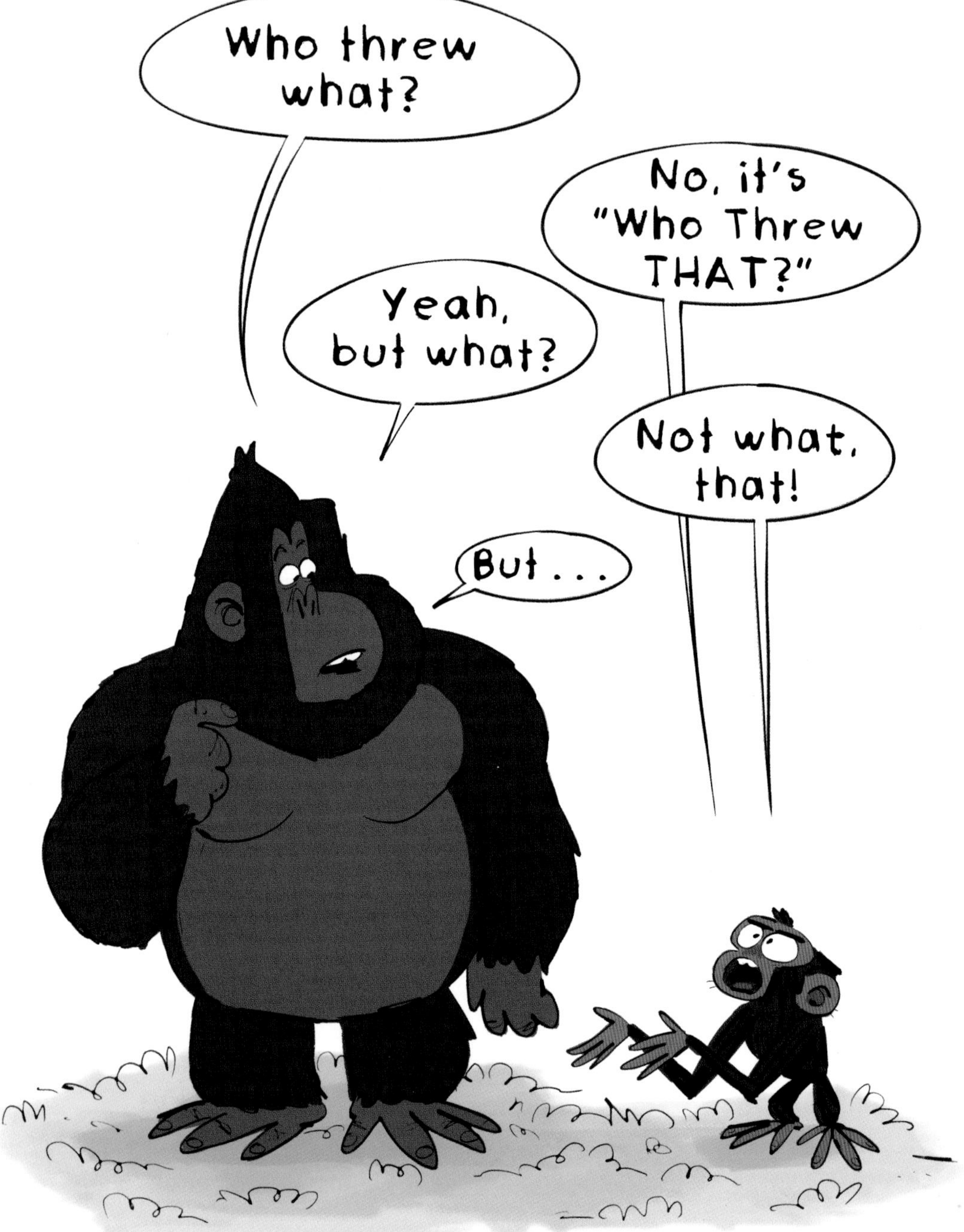
Who threw what?
Yeah, but what?
No, it's "Who Threw THAT?"
Not what, that!
But . . .

CONTENTS

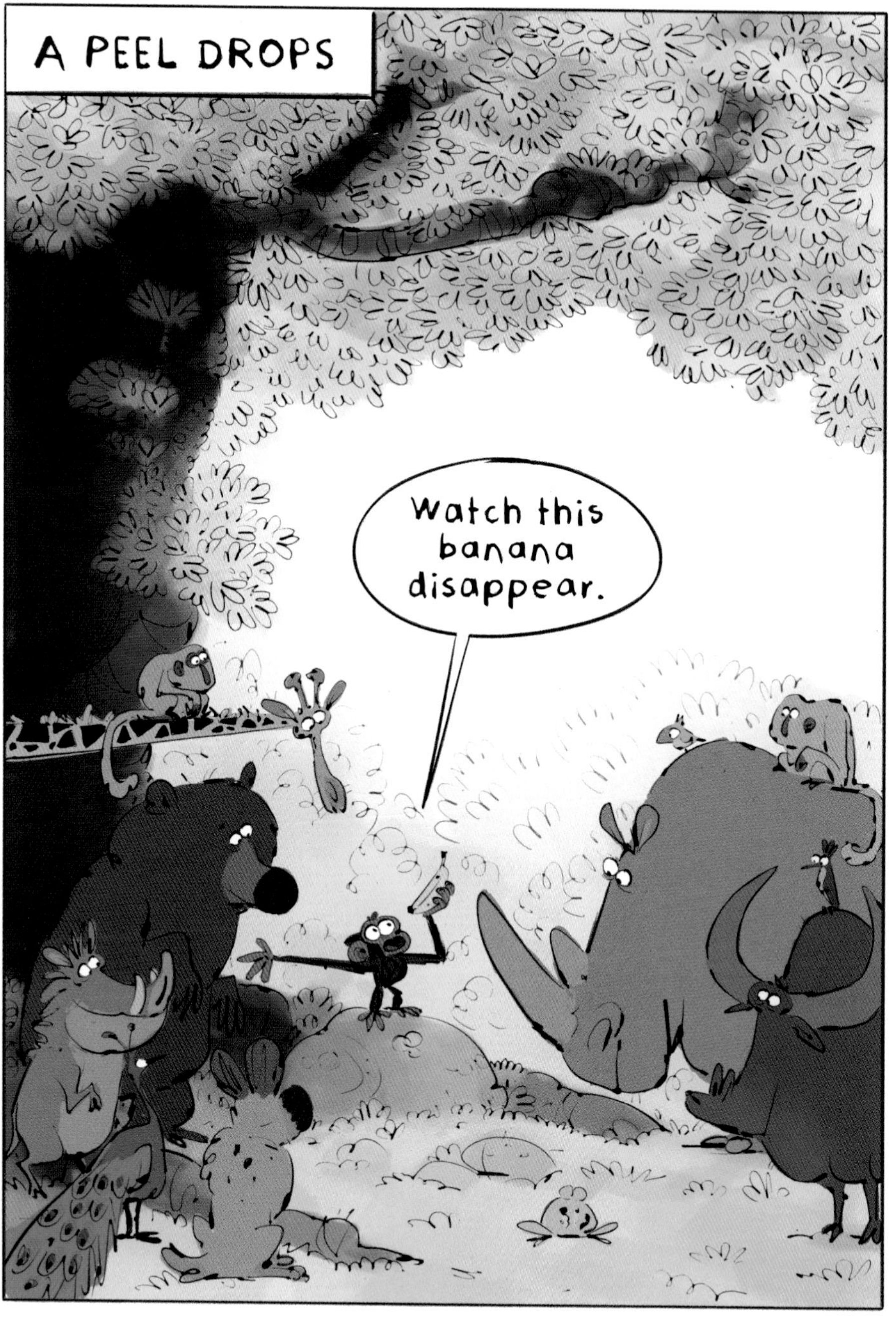
A PEEL DROPS
Watch this banana disappear.

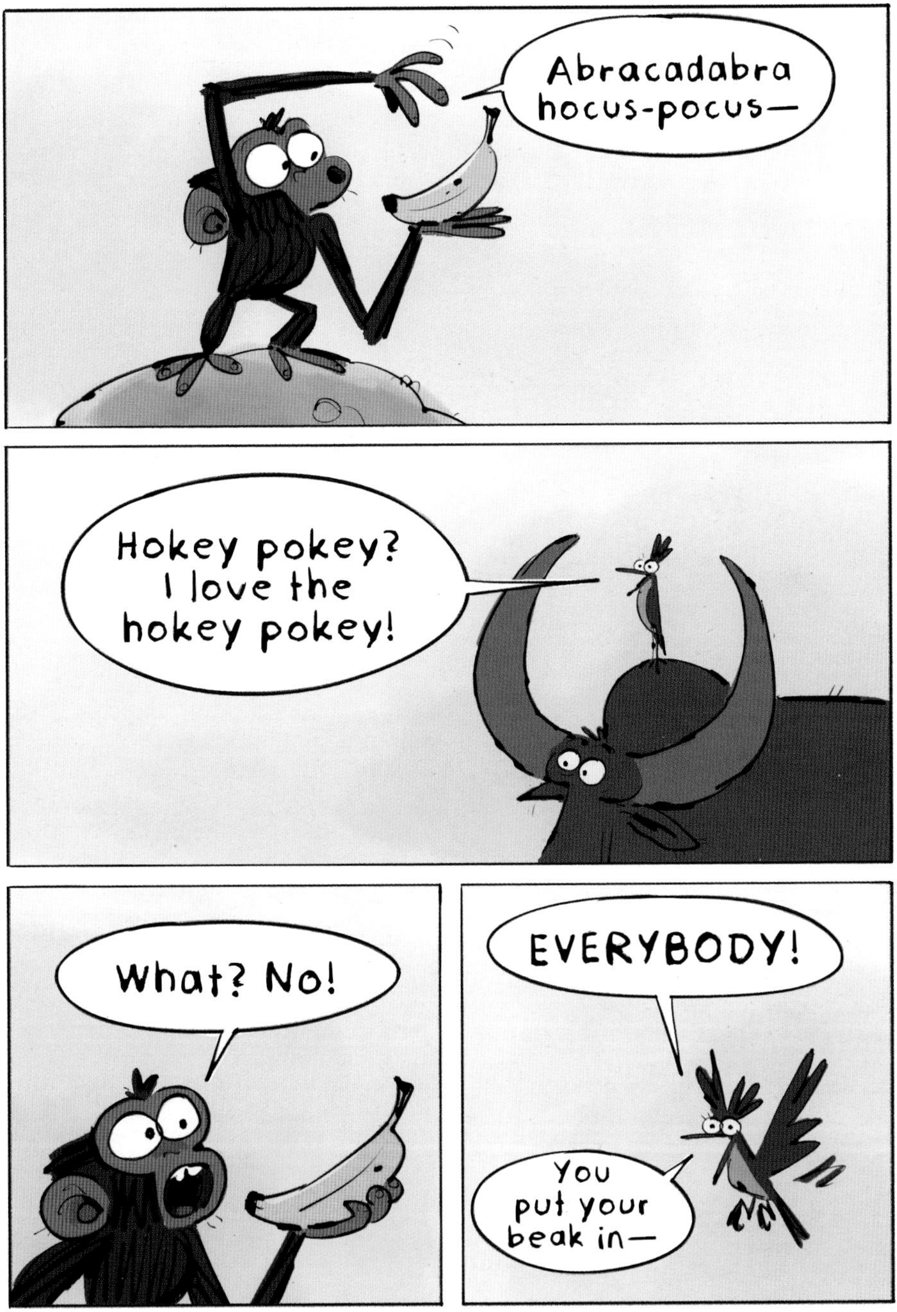
Abracadabra hocus-pocus—
Hokey pokey? I love the hokey pokey!
What? No!
EVERYBODY!
You put your beak in—

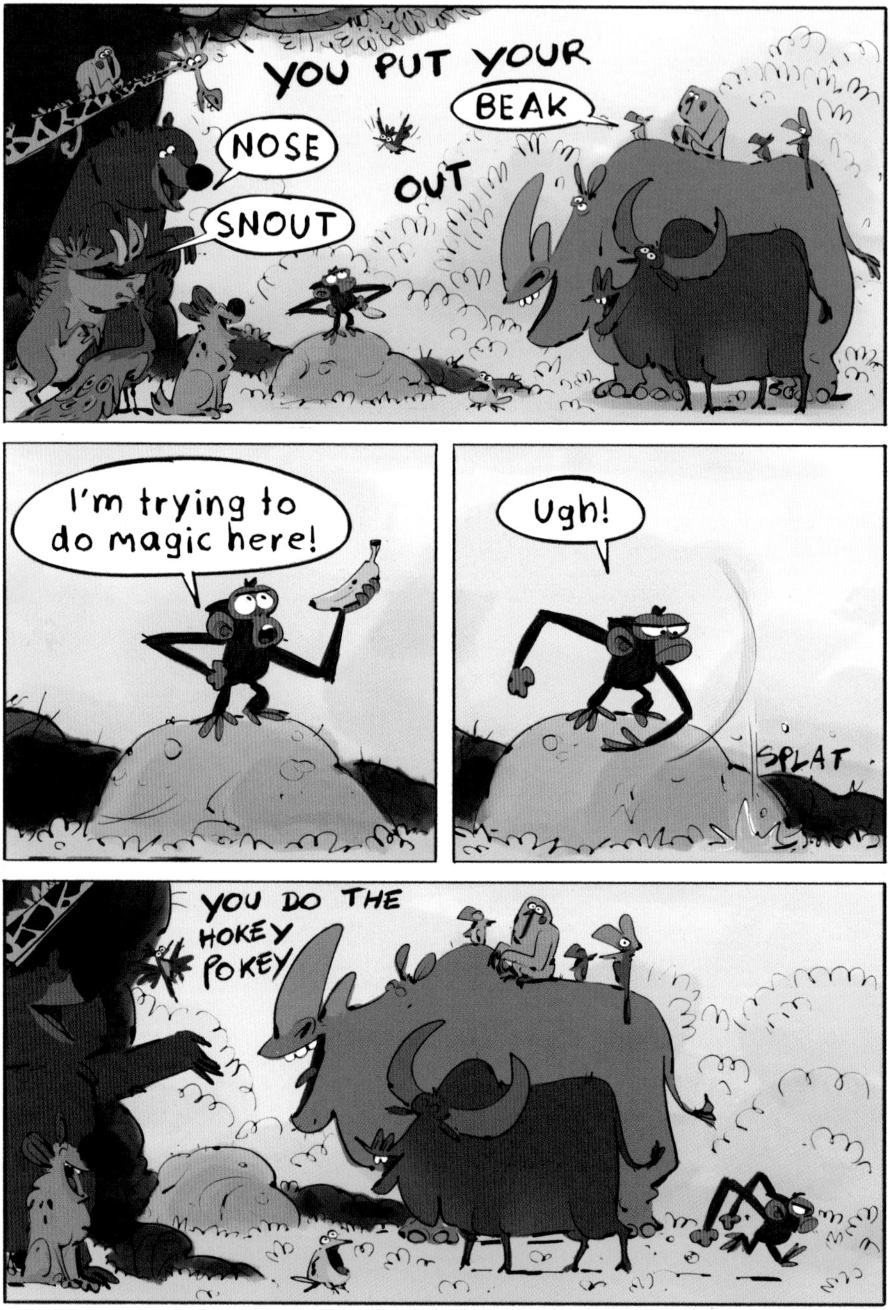
YOU PUT YOUR
NOSE
BEAK
SNOUT
OUT
I'm trying to do magic here!
Ugh!
SPLAT
YOU DO THE HOKEY POKEY

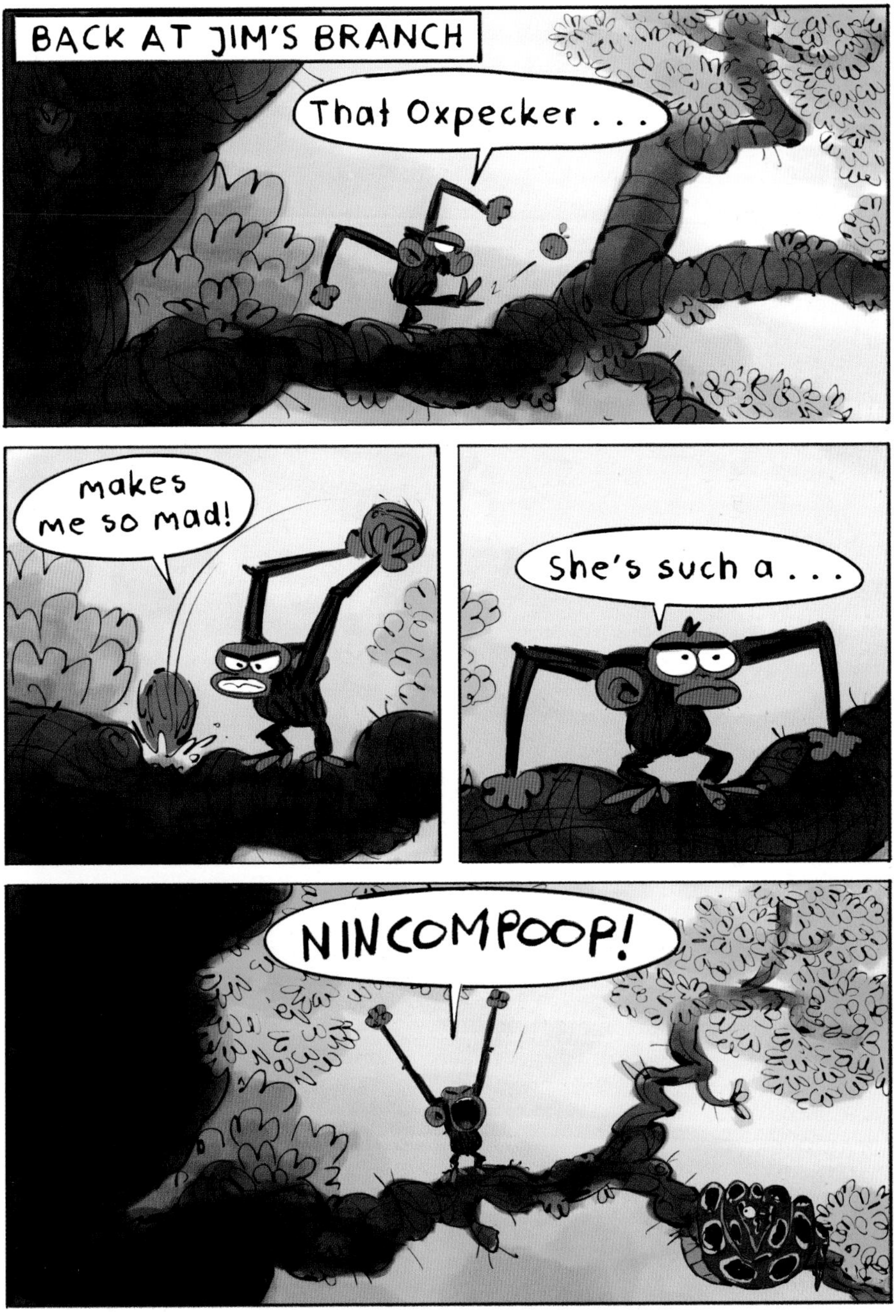
BACK AT JIM'S BRANCH
That Oxpecker . . .
makes me so mad!
She's such a . . .
NINCOMPOOP!

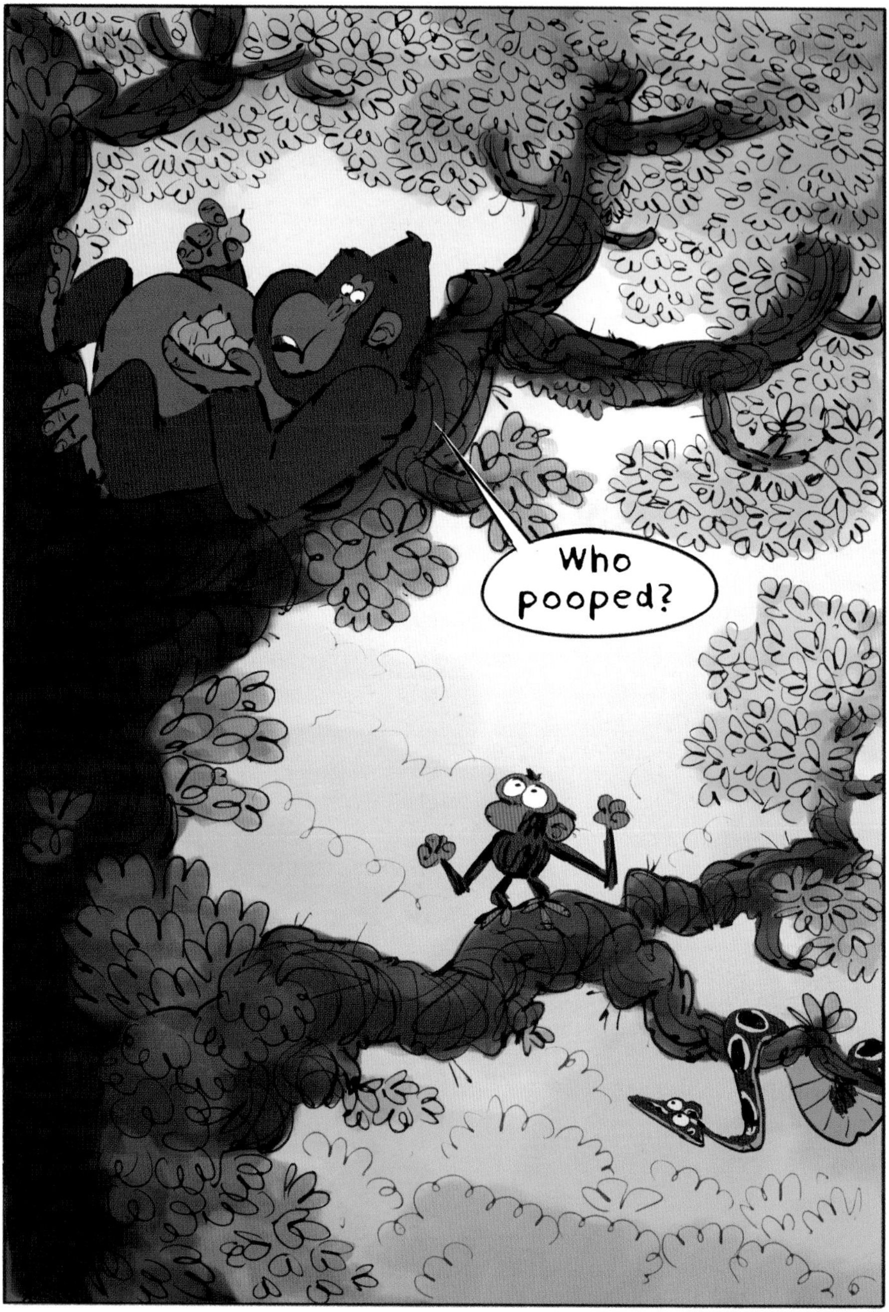
Who pooped?

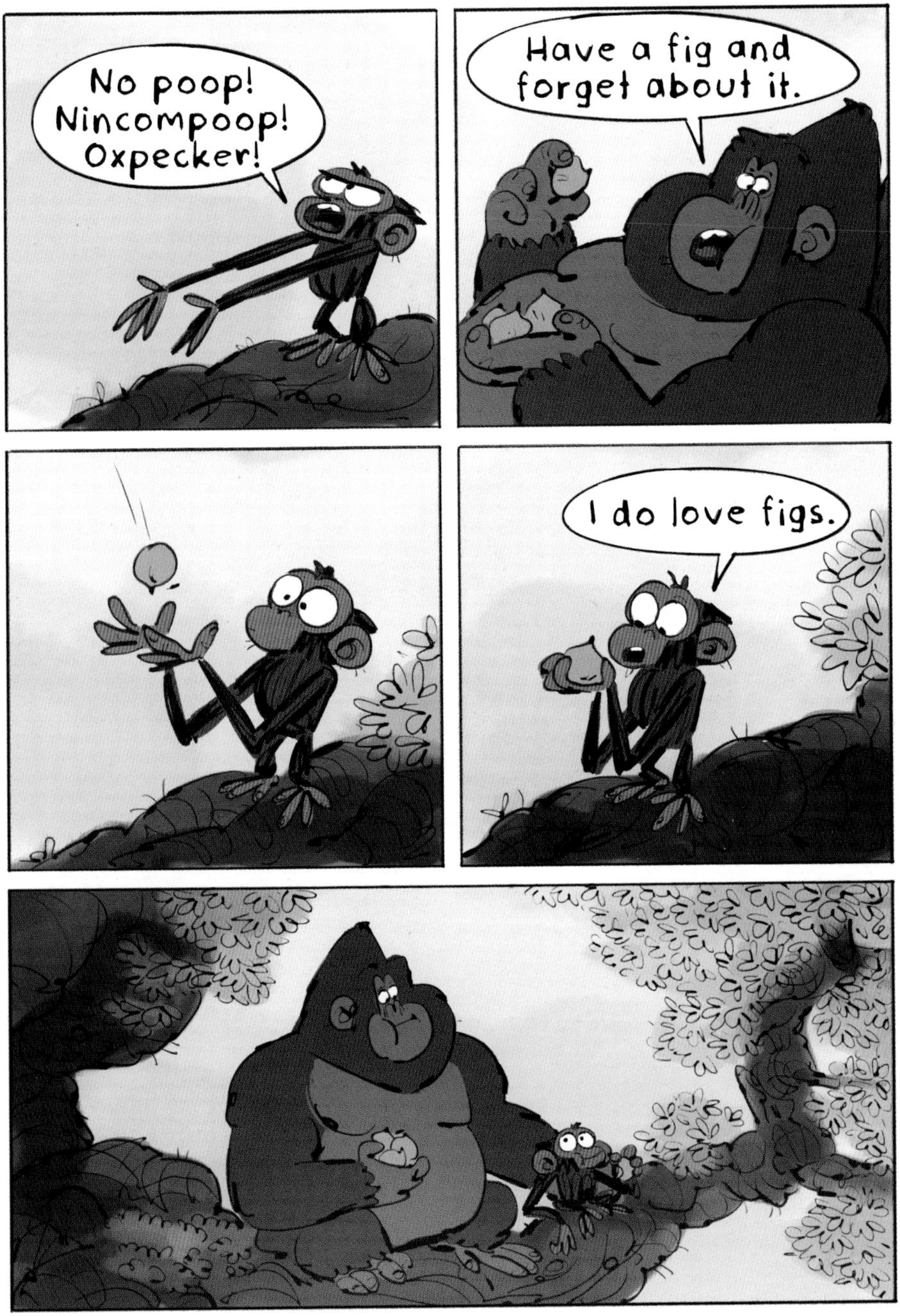
No poop! Nincompoop! Oxpecker!
Have a fig and forget about it.
I do love figs.

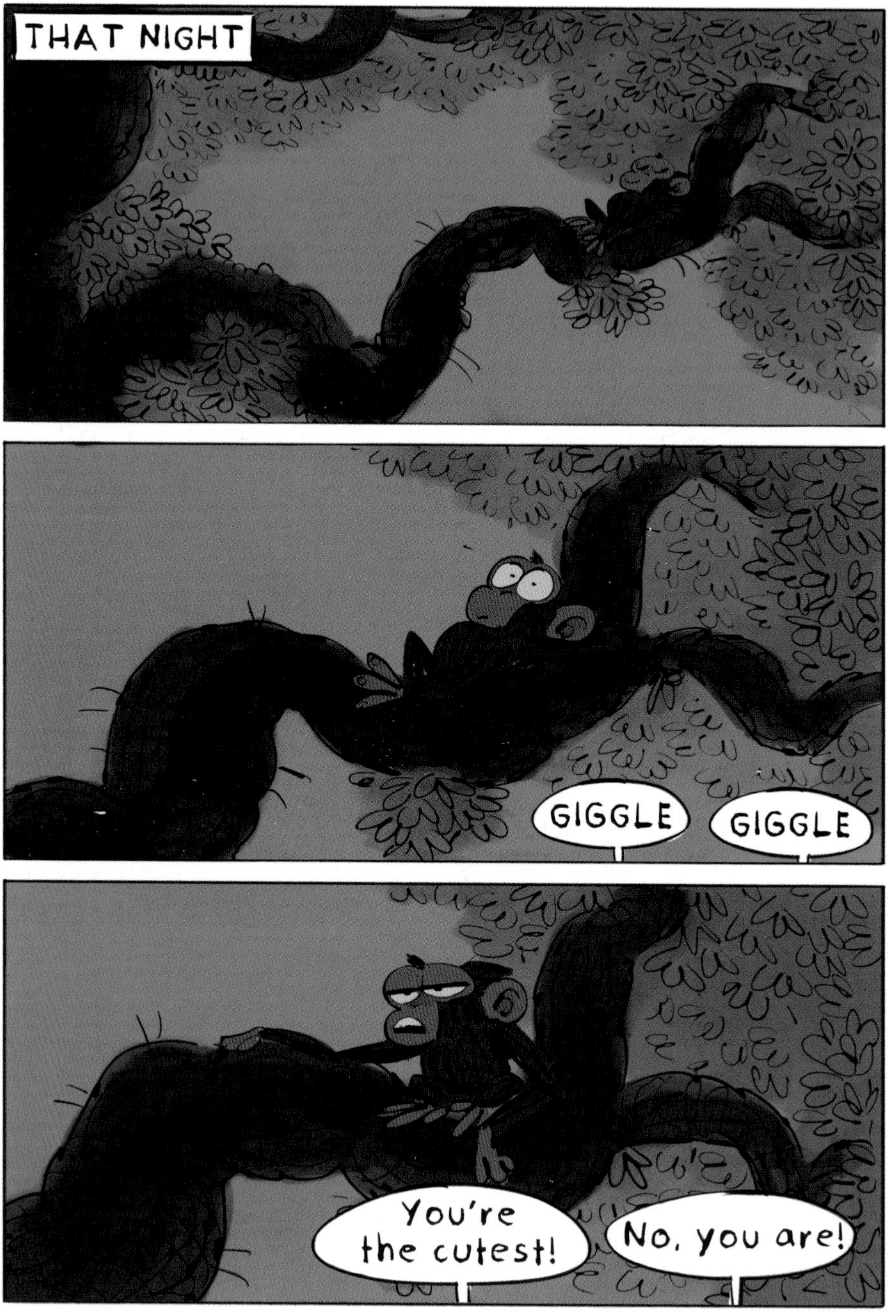
THAT NIGHT
GIGGLE
GIGGLE
You're the cutest!
No, you are!

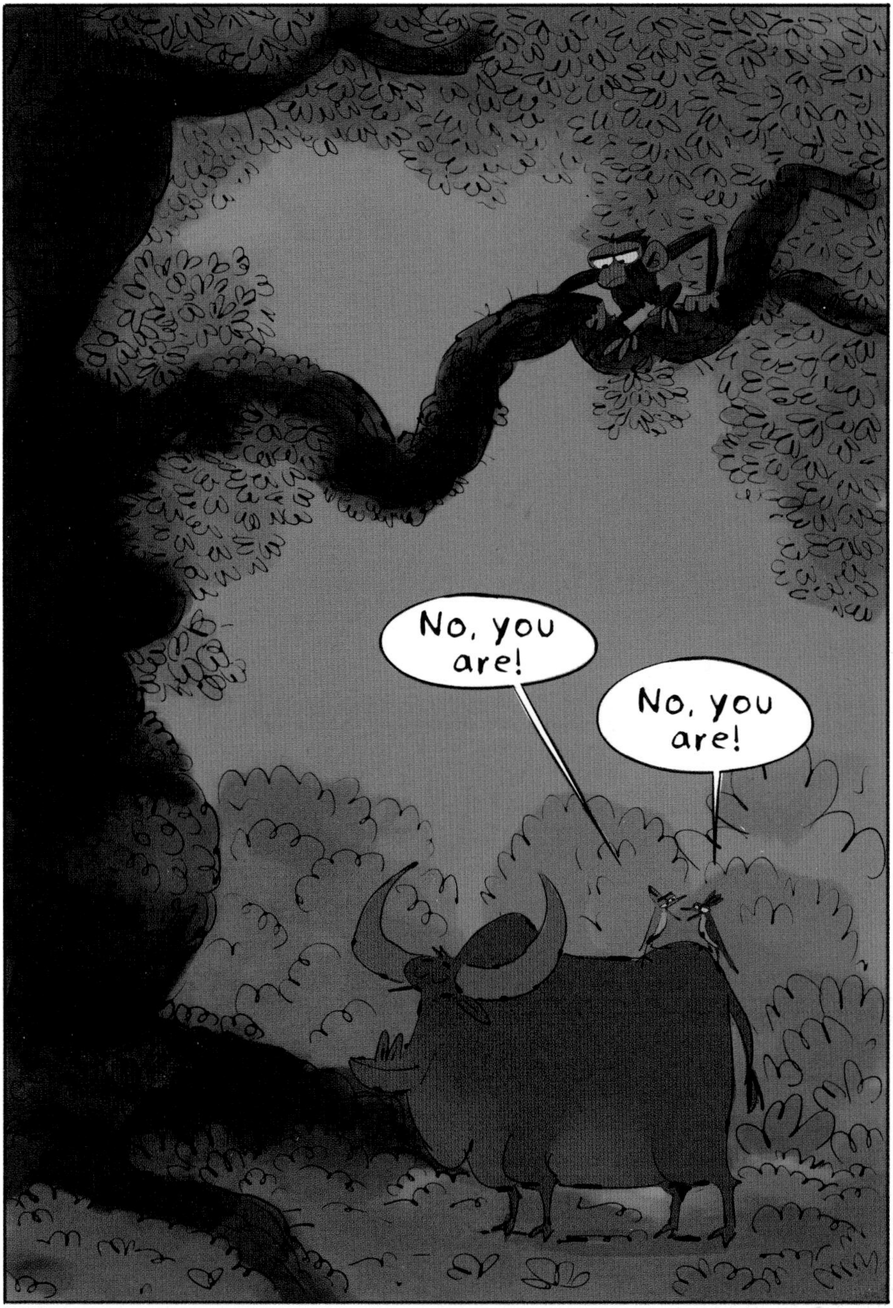
No, you are!
No, you are!

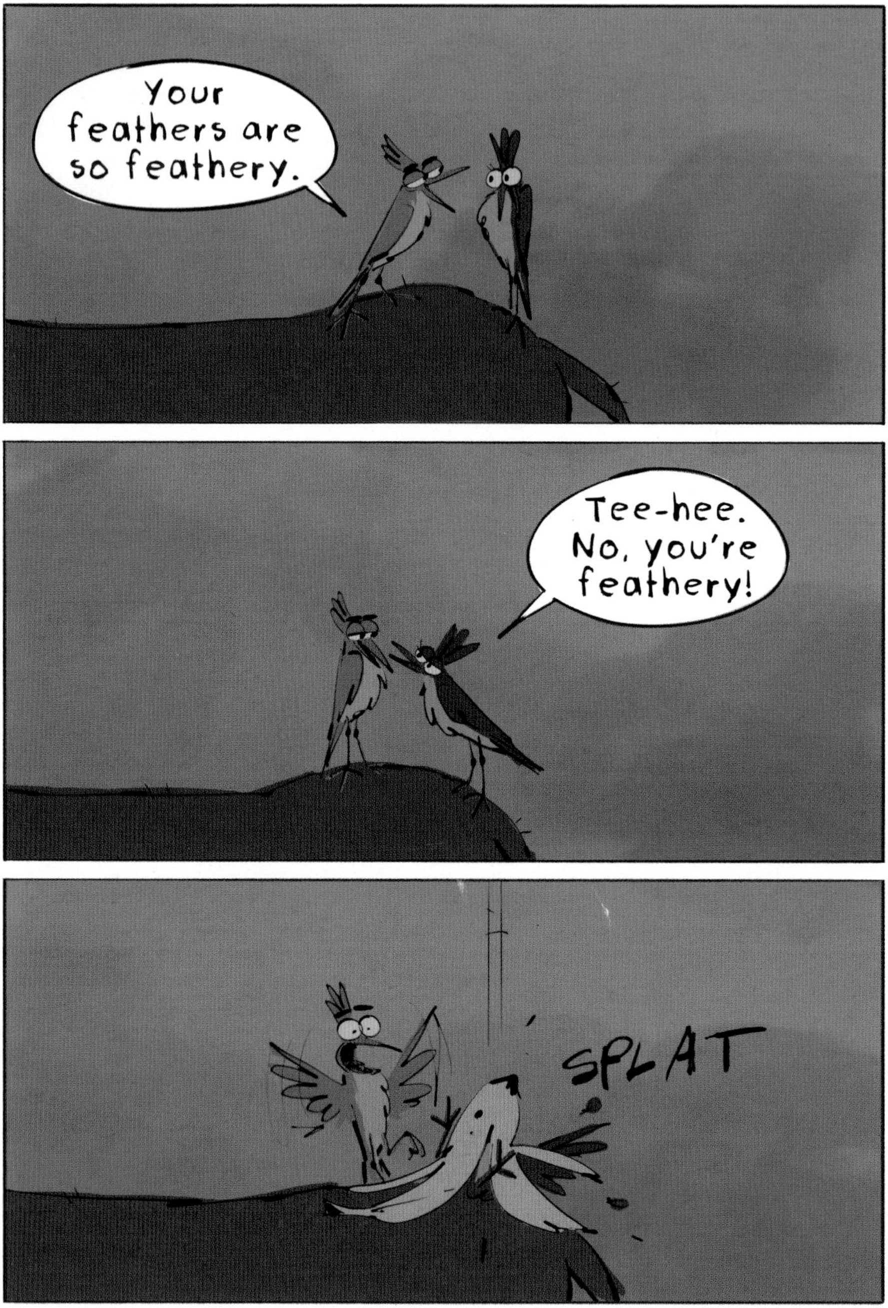
Your feathers are so feathery.
Tee-hee. No, you're feathery!
SPLAT

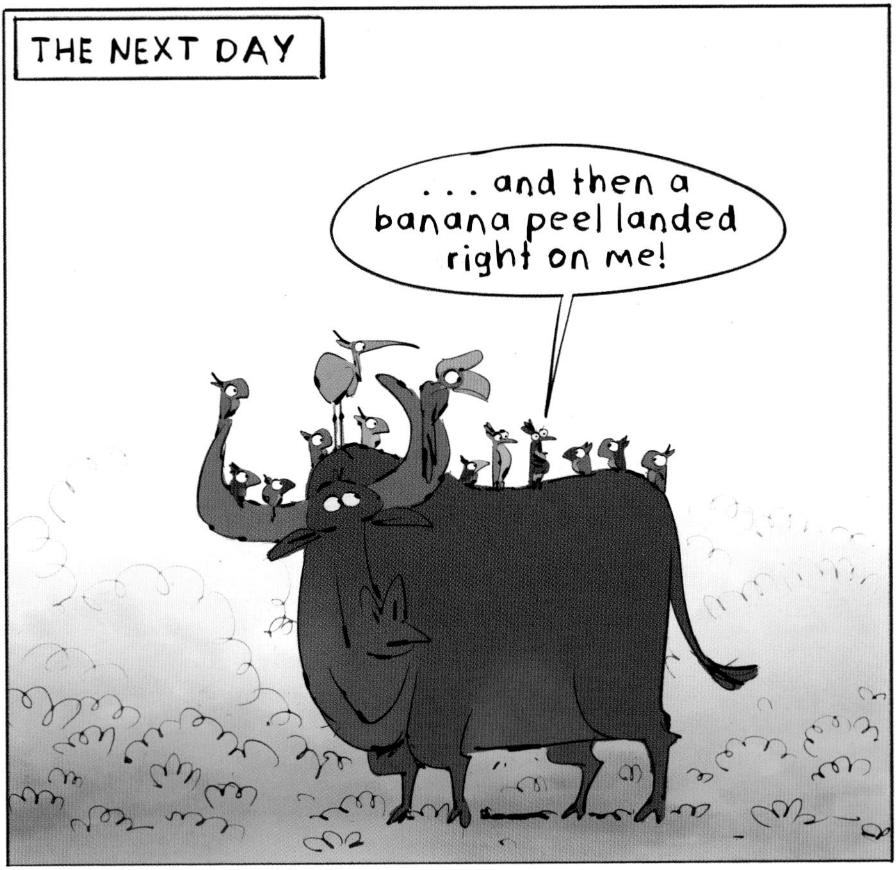
THE NEXT DAY
. . . and then a banana peel landed right on me!

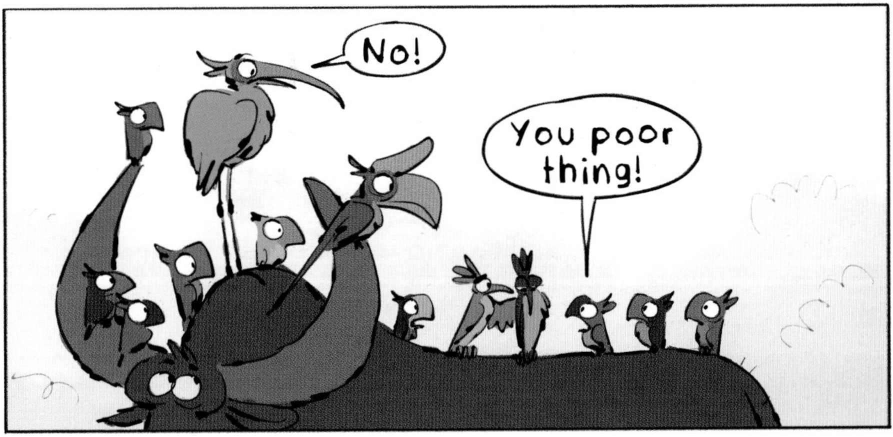
No!
You poor thing!

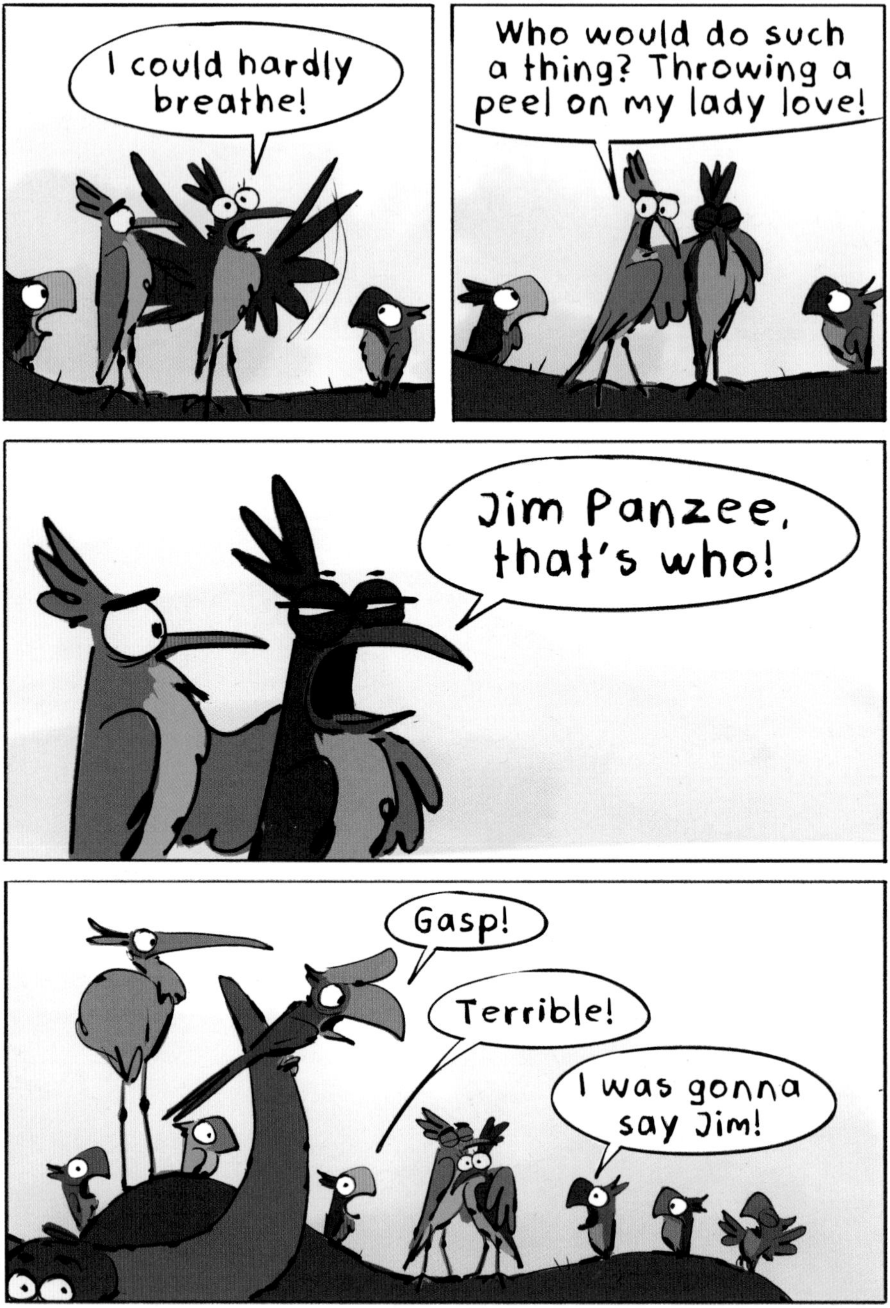
I could hardly breathe!
Who would do such a thing? Throwing a peel on my lady love!
Jim Panzee, that's who!
Gasp!
Terrible!
I was gonna say Jim!

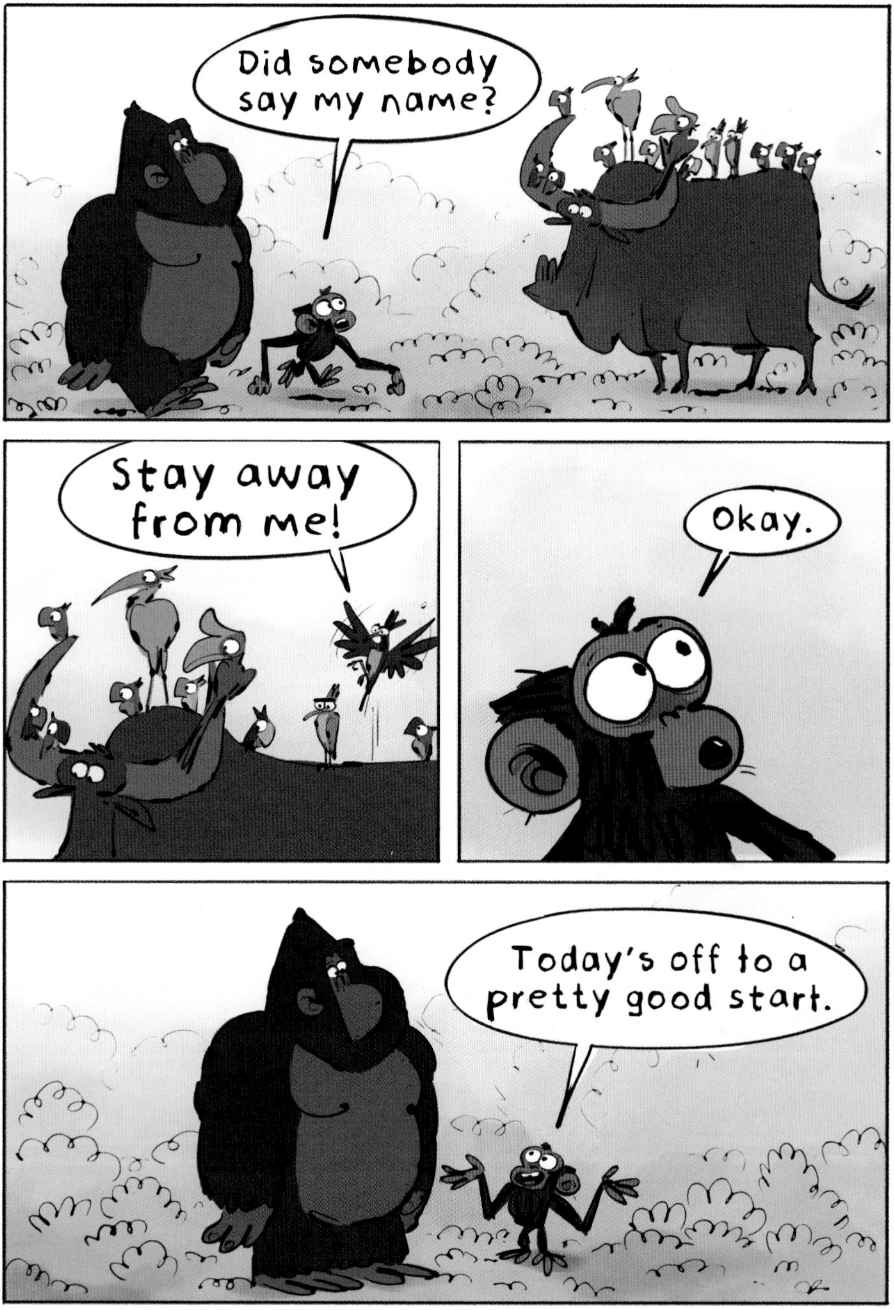
Did somebody say my name?
Stay away from me!
Okay.
Today's off to a pretty good start.

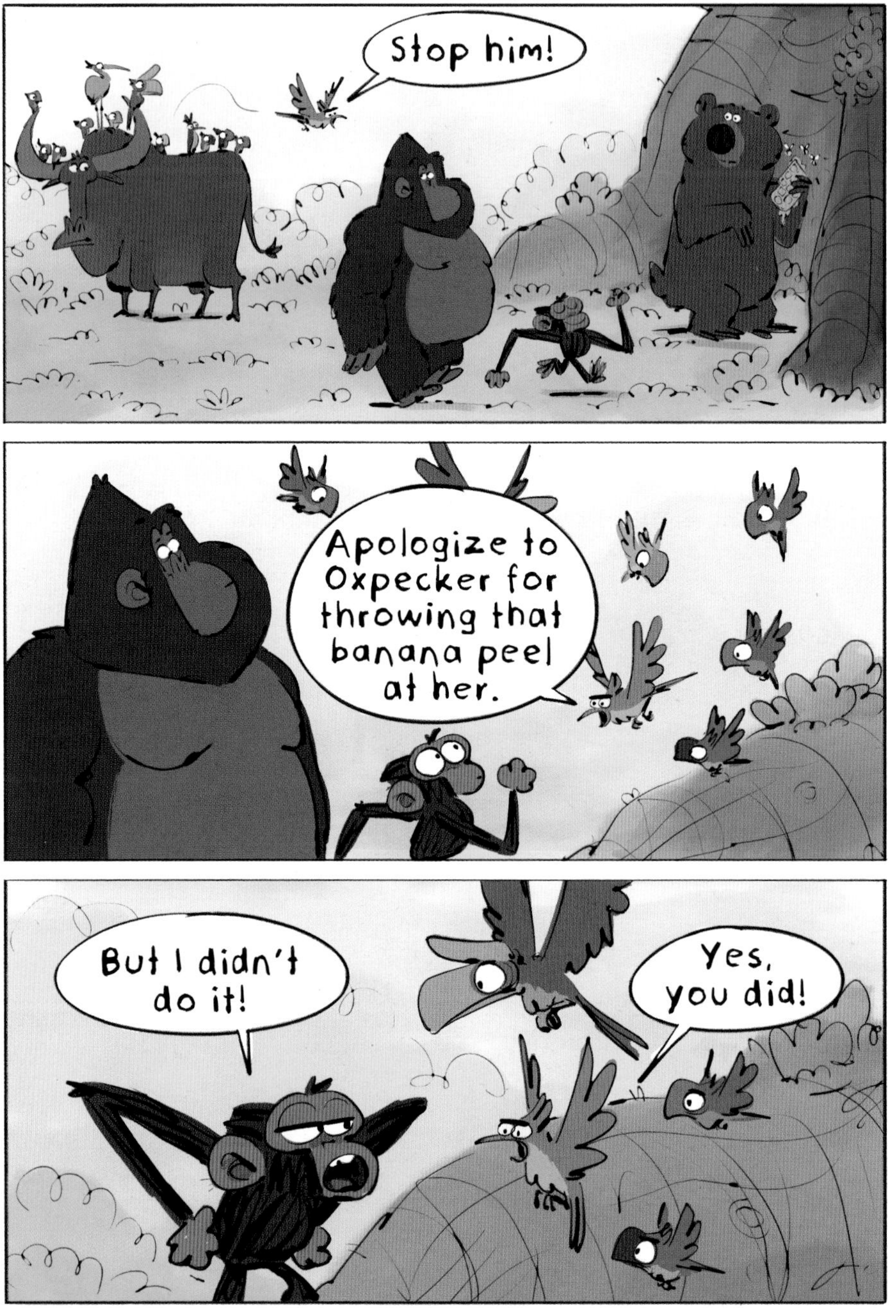
Stop him!
Apologize to Oxpecker for throwing that banana peel at her.
But I didn't do it!
Yes, you did!

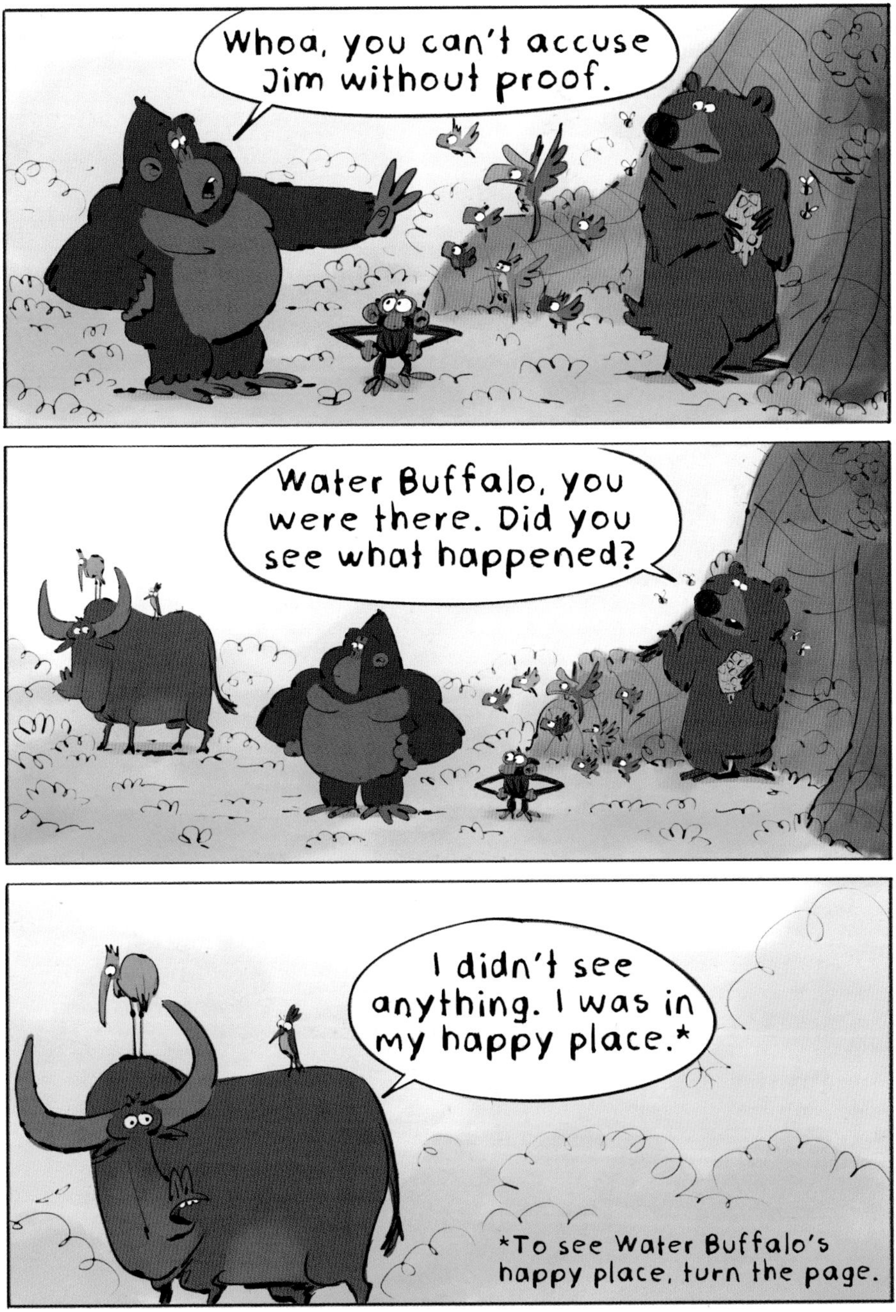
Whoa, you can't accuse Jim without proof.
Water Buffalo, you were there. Did you see what happened?
I didn't see anything. I was in my happy place.*
*To see Water Buffalo's happy place, turn the page.

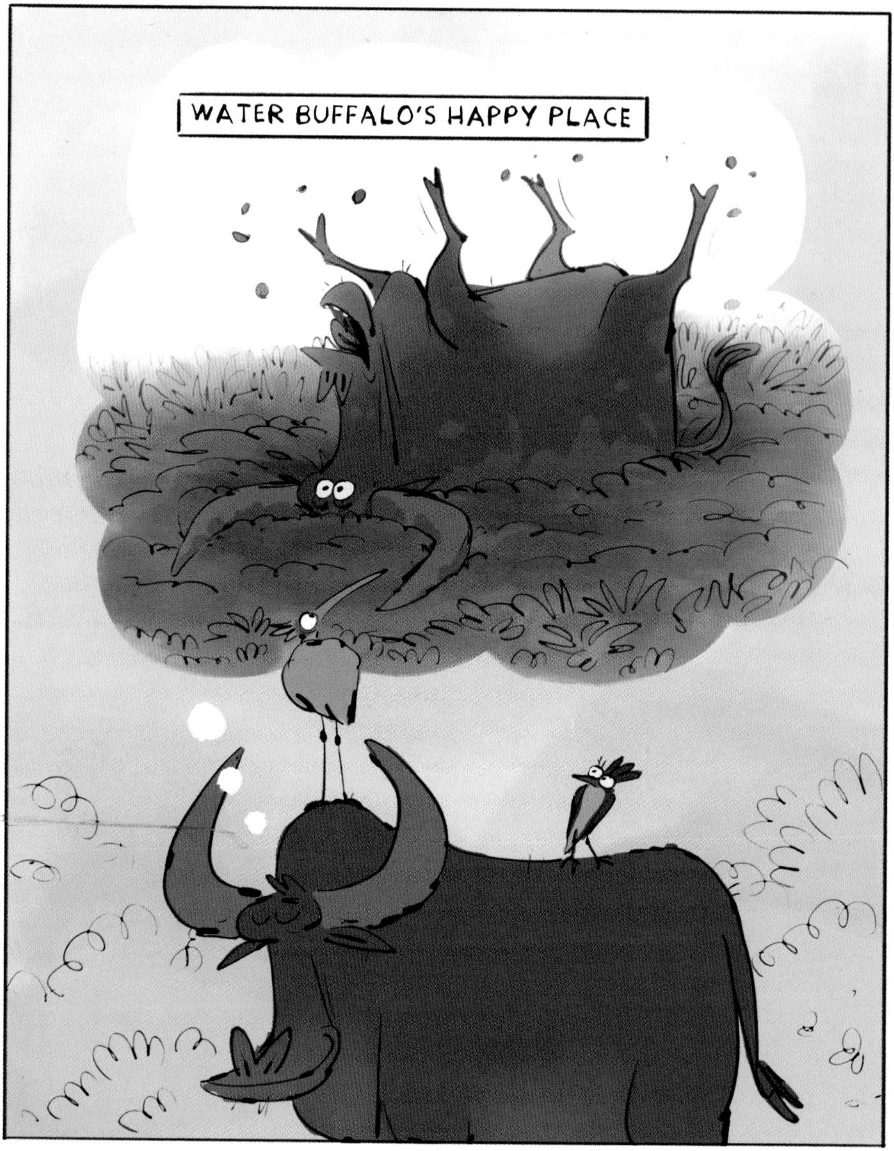
WATER BUFFALO'S HAPPY PLACE

(A happy place is something you imagine that makes you happy. It can be helpful to go to the happy place in your imagination when you feel stressed, upset, or in Water Buffalo's case, totally grossed out.)

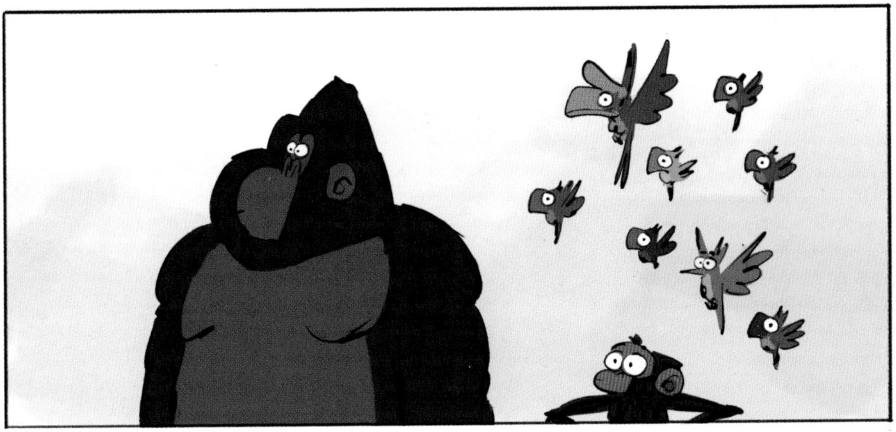

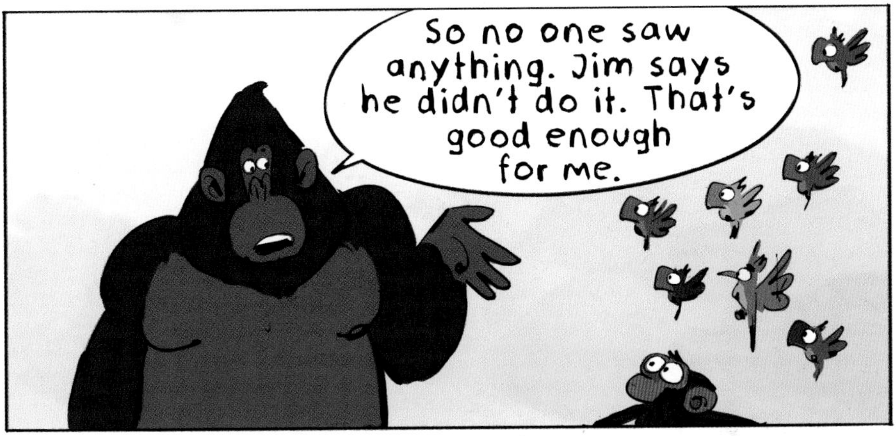
So no one saw anything. Jim says he didn't do it. That's good enough for me.

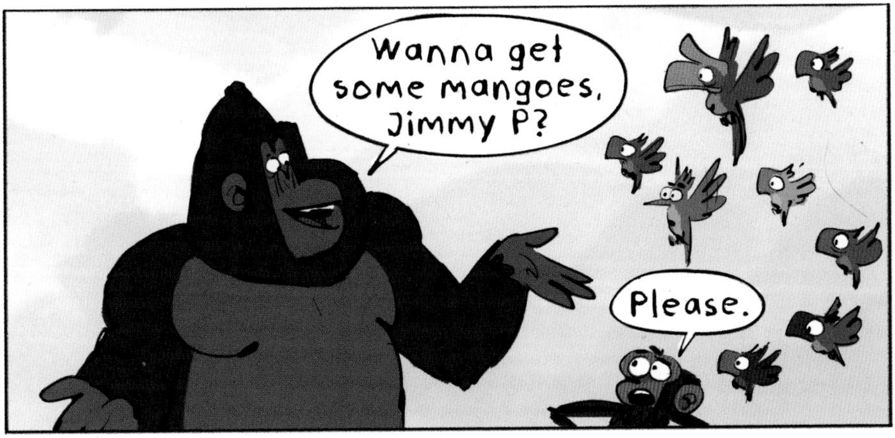
Wanna get some mangoes, Jimmy P?
Please.

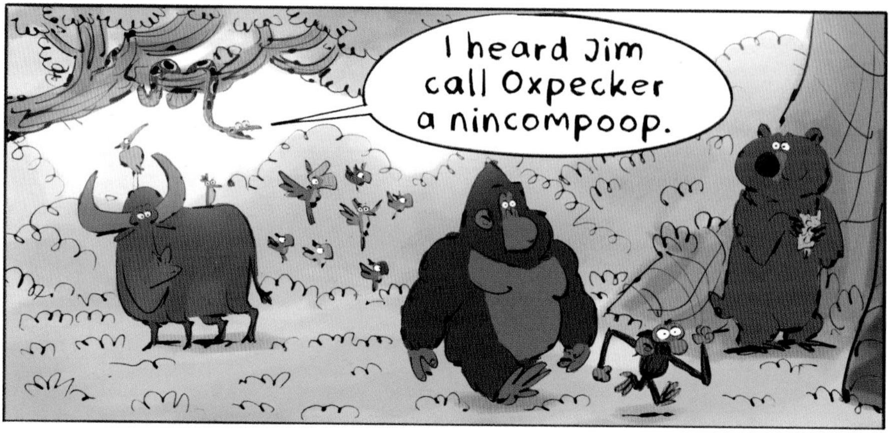
I heard Jim call Oxpecker a nincompoop.

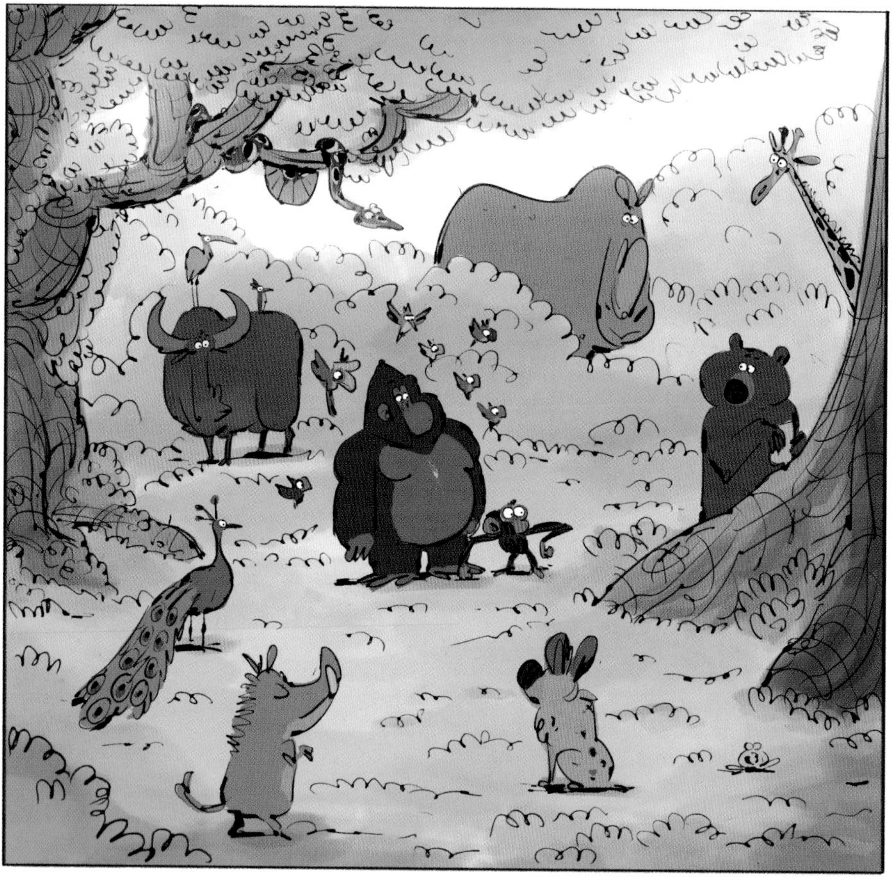

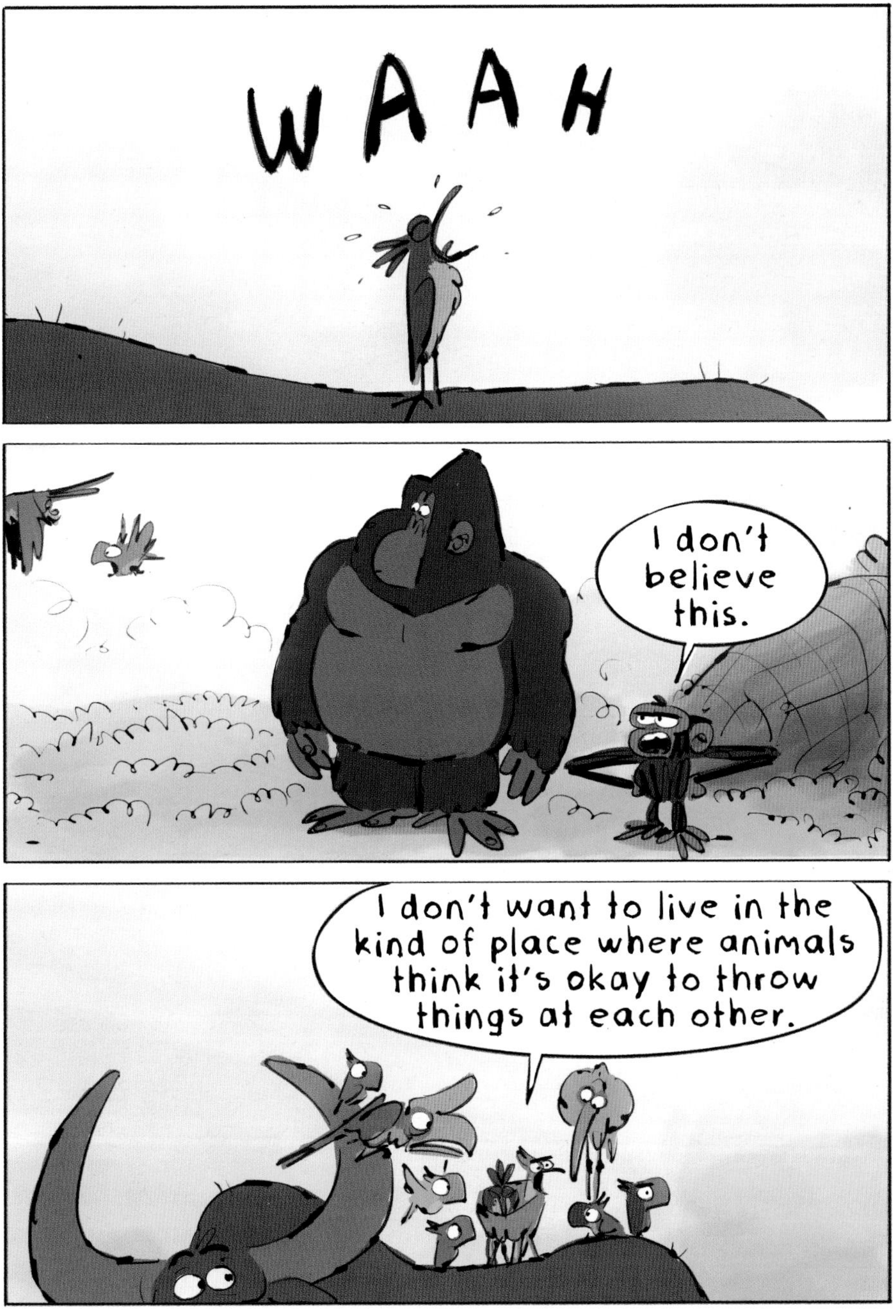
WAAH
I don't believe this.
I don't want to live in the kind of place where animals think it's okay to throw things at each other.

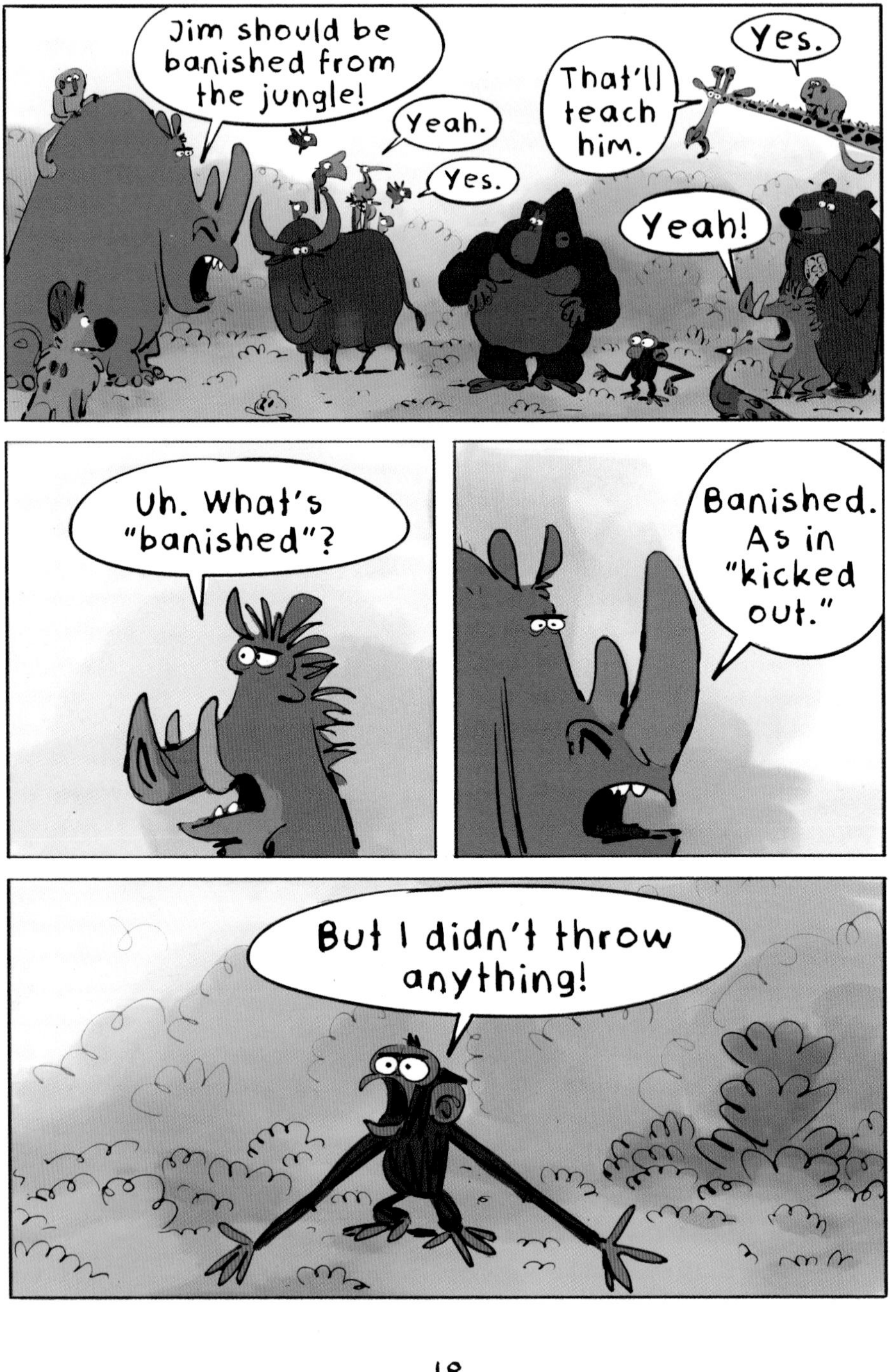
Jim should be banished from the jungle!
Yeah.
Yes.
That'll teach him.
Yes.
Yeah!
Uh. What's "banished"?
Banished. As in "kicked out."
But I didn't throw anything!

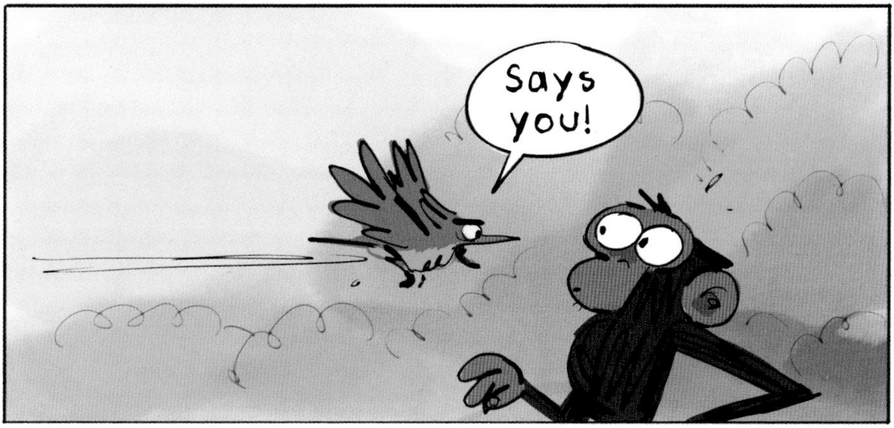
Says you!

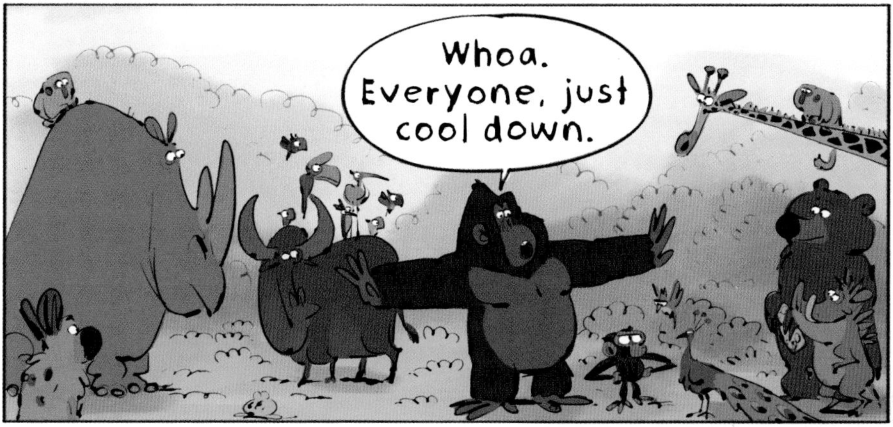
Whoa. Everyone, just cool down.

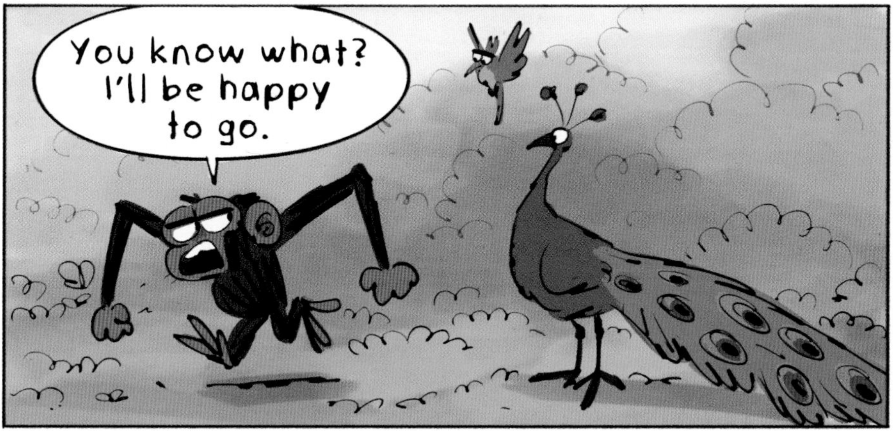
You know what? I'll be happy to go.

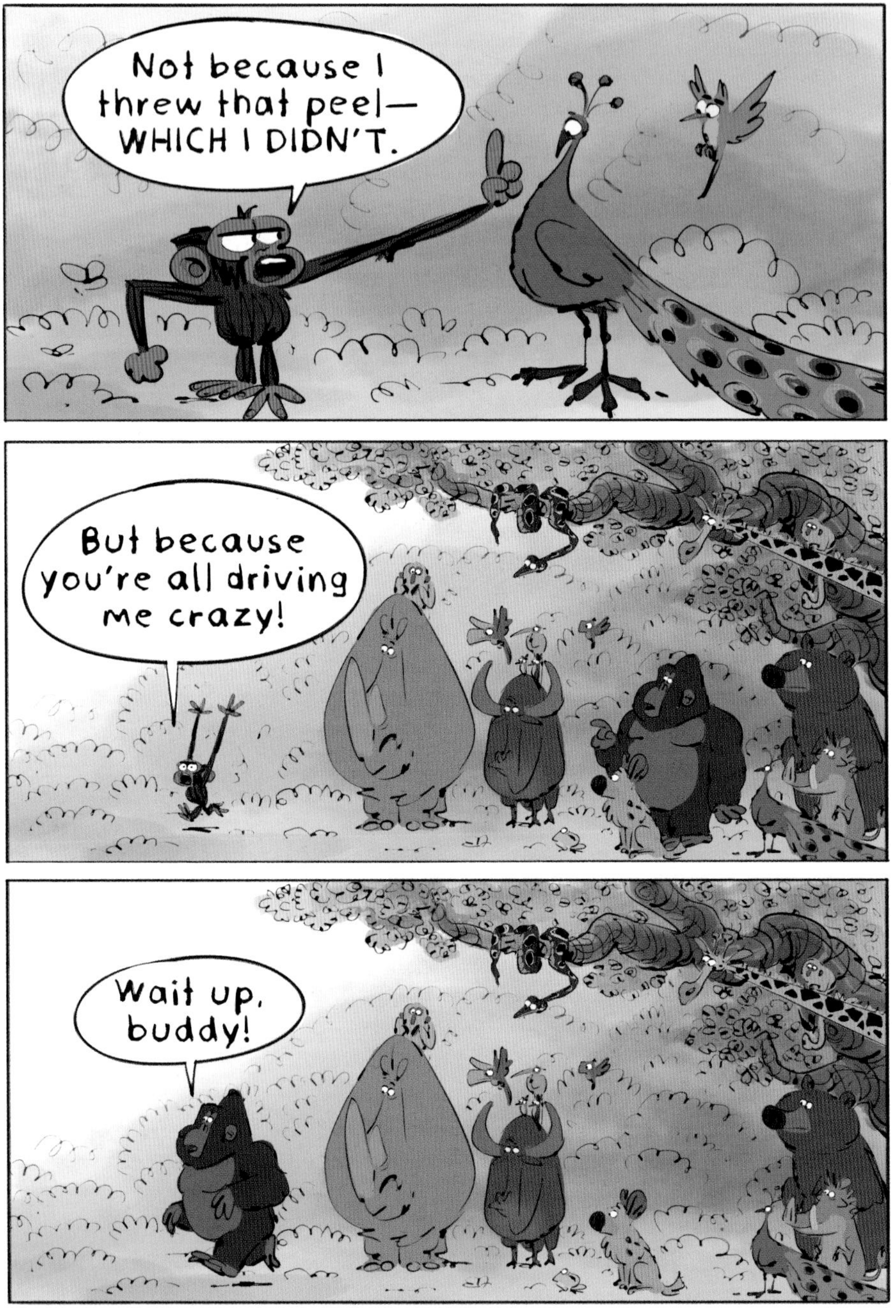
Not because I threw that peel—WHICH I DIDN'T.
But because you're all driving me crazy!
Wait up, buddy!

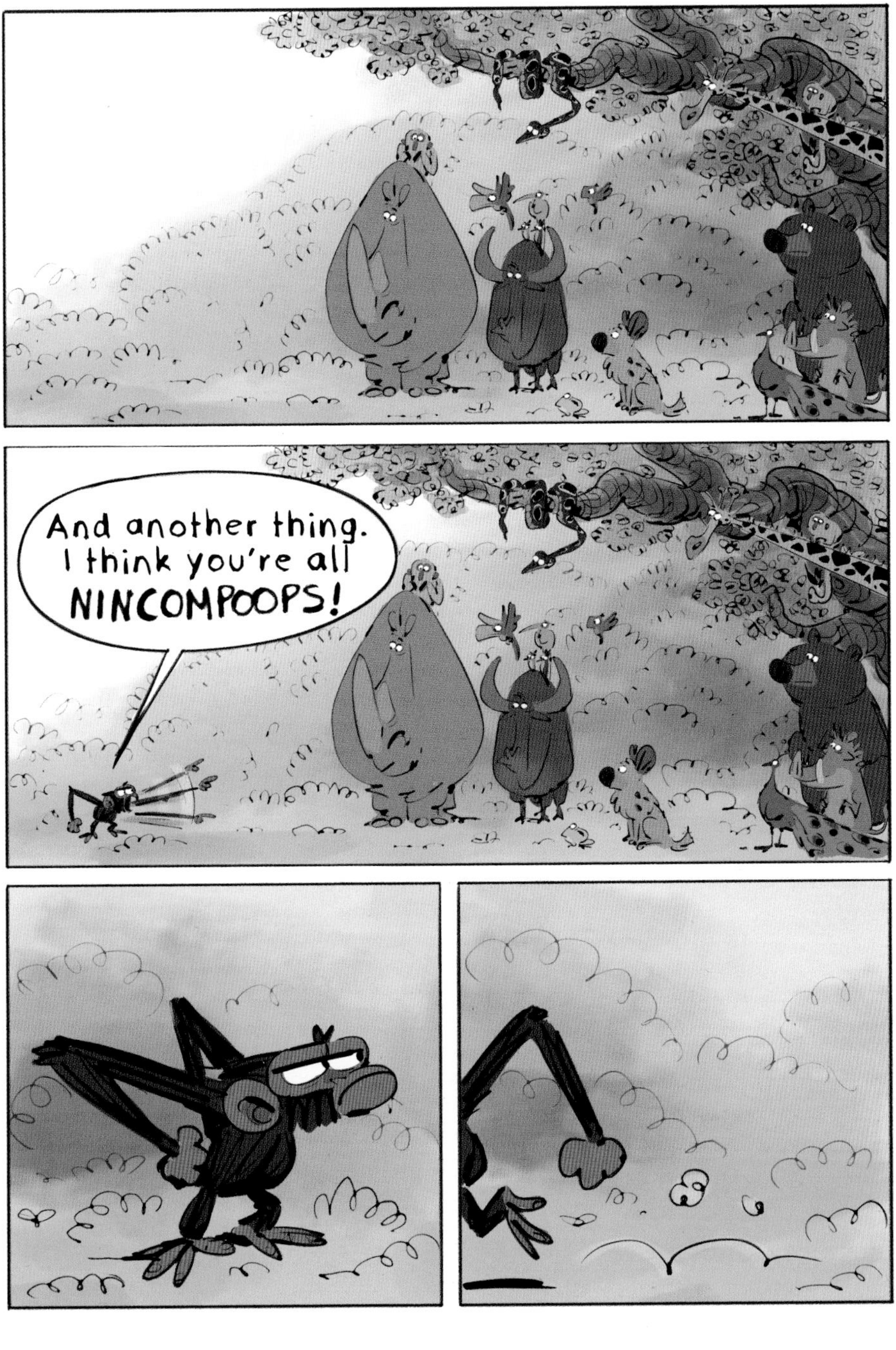
And another thing. I think you're all NINCOMPOOPS!

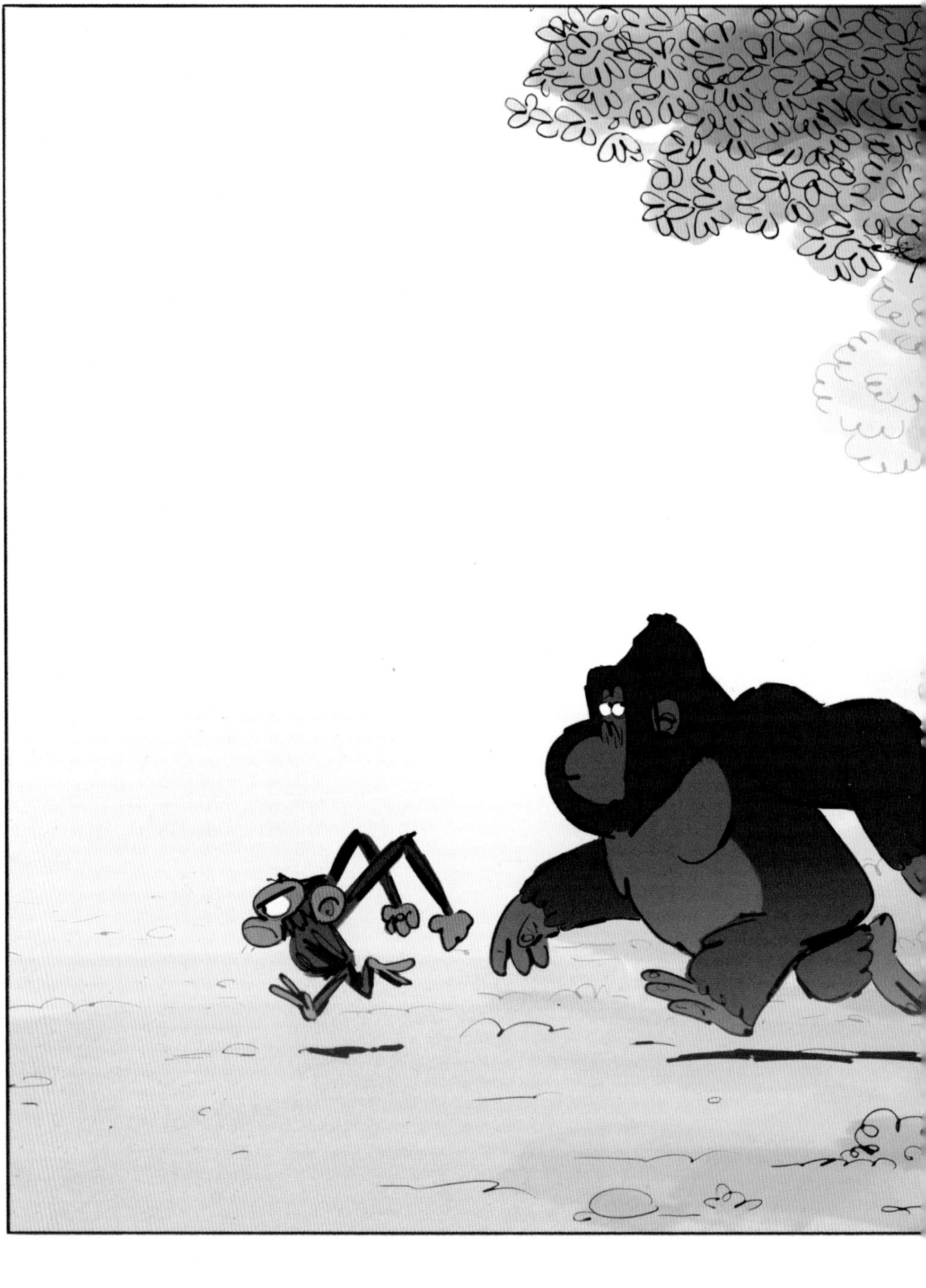

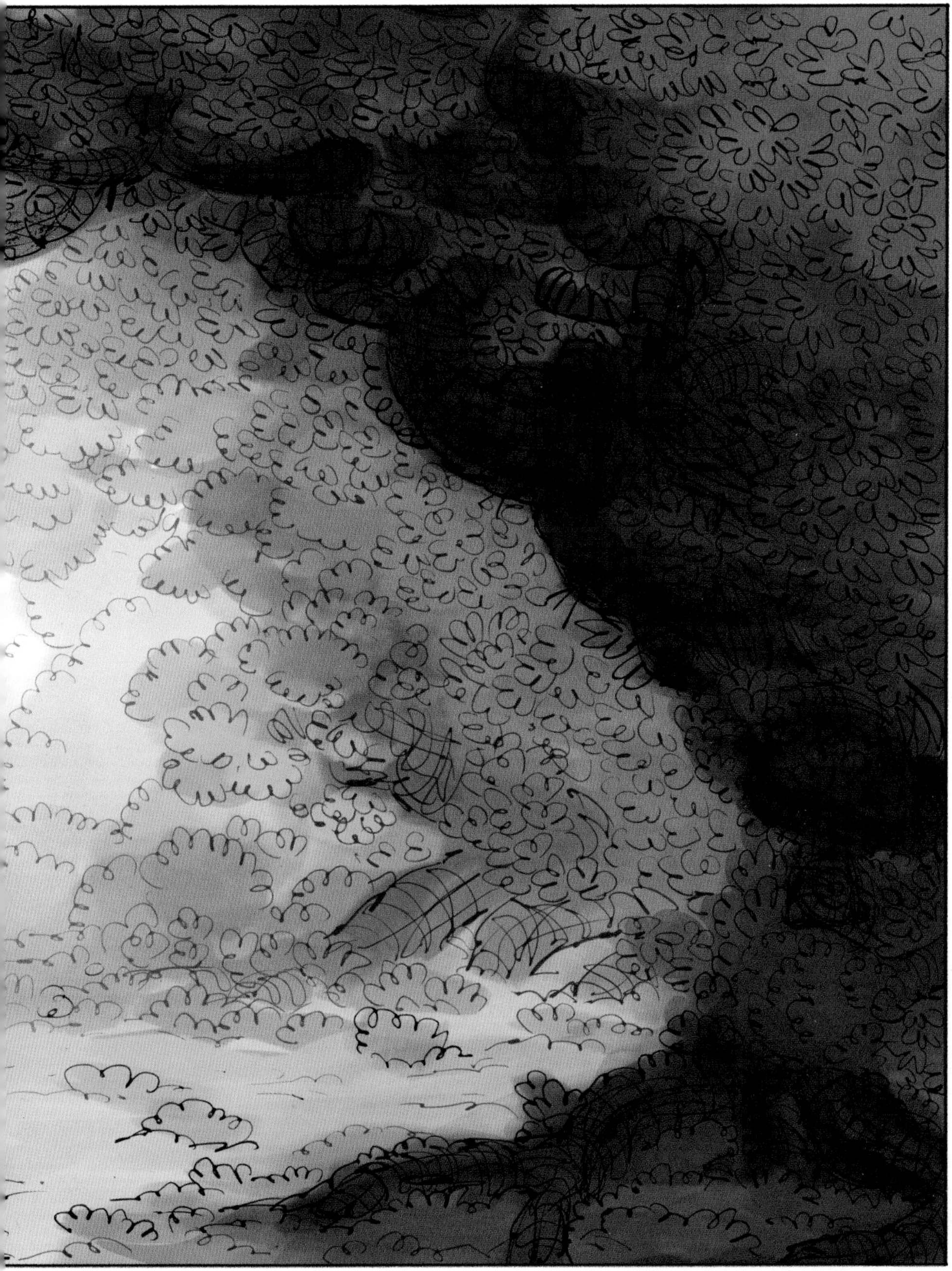

TO BE CONTINUED

PAM PANZEE'S PRIMATE PRIMER

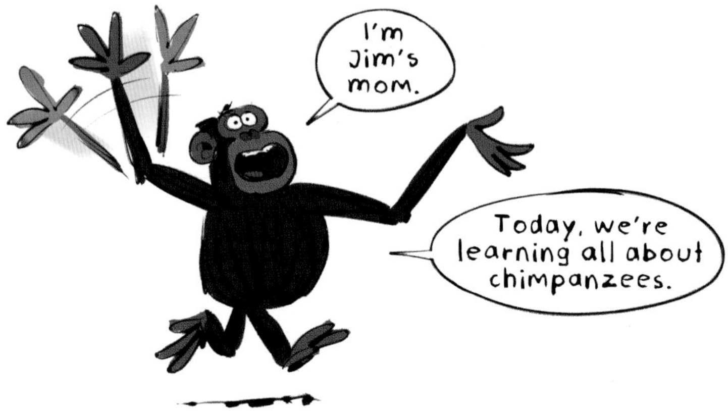
I'm Jim's mom.
Today, we're learning all about chimpanzees.

Chimpanzees are one of the great apes.
The other great apes are:

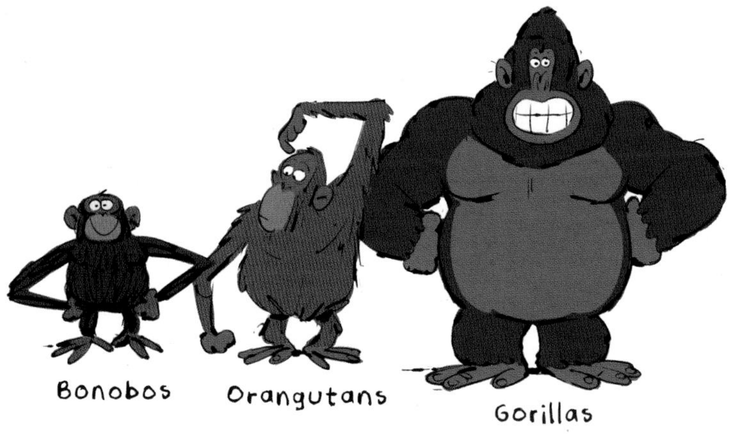
Bonobos
Orangutans
Gorillas

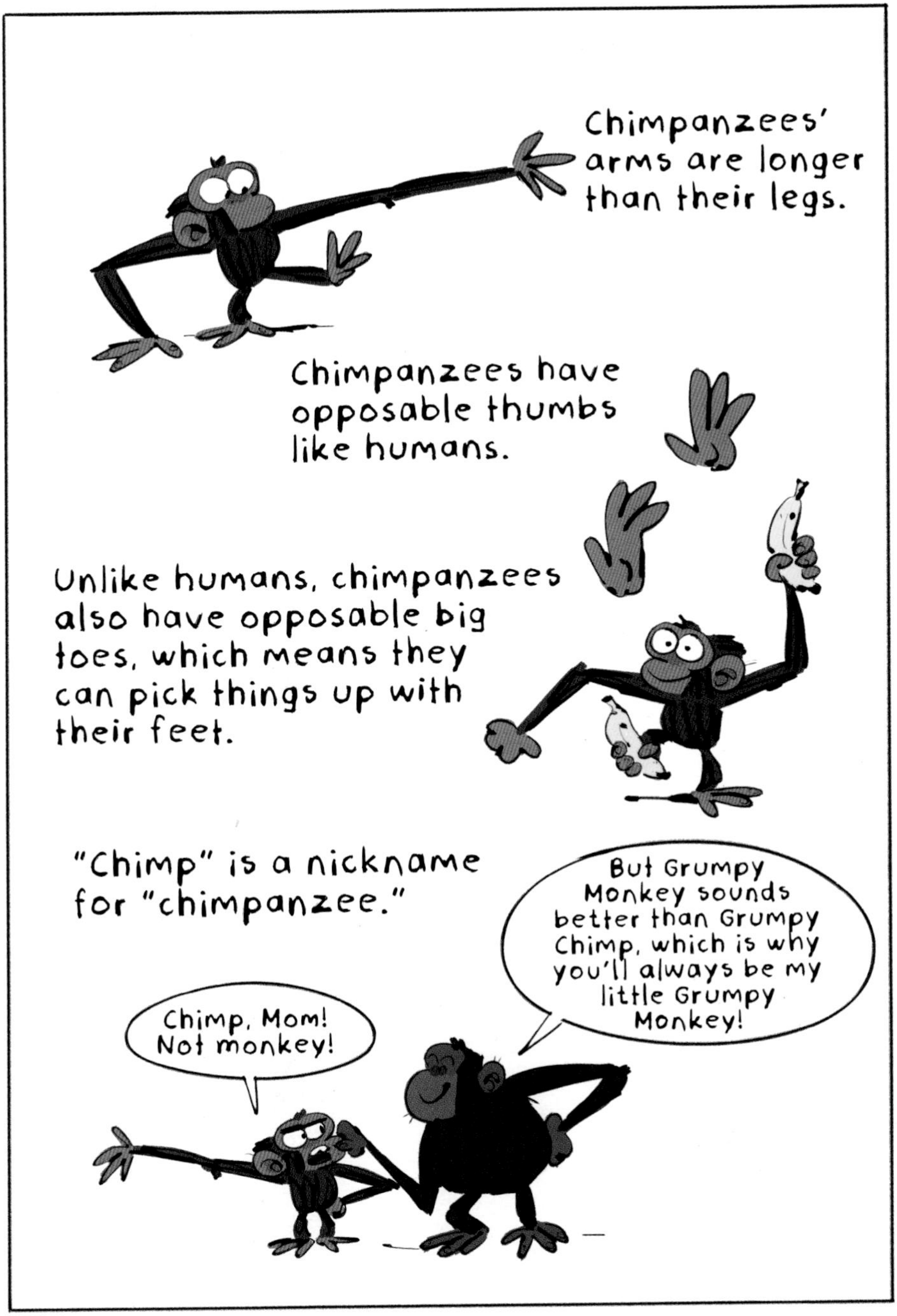
Chimpanzees' arms are longer than their legs.
Chimpanzees have opposable thumbs like humans.
Unlike humans, chimpanzees also have opposable big toes, which means they can pick things up with their feet.
"Chimp" is a nickname for "chimpanzee."
But Grumpy Monkey sounds better than Grumpy Chimp, which is why you'll always be my little Grumpy Monkey!
Chimp, Mom! Not monkey!

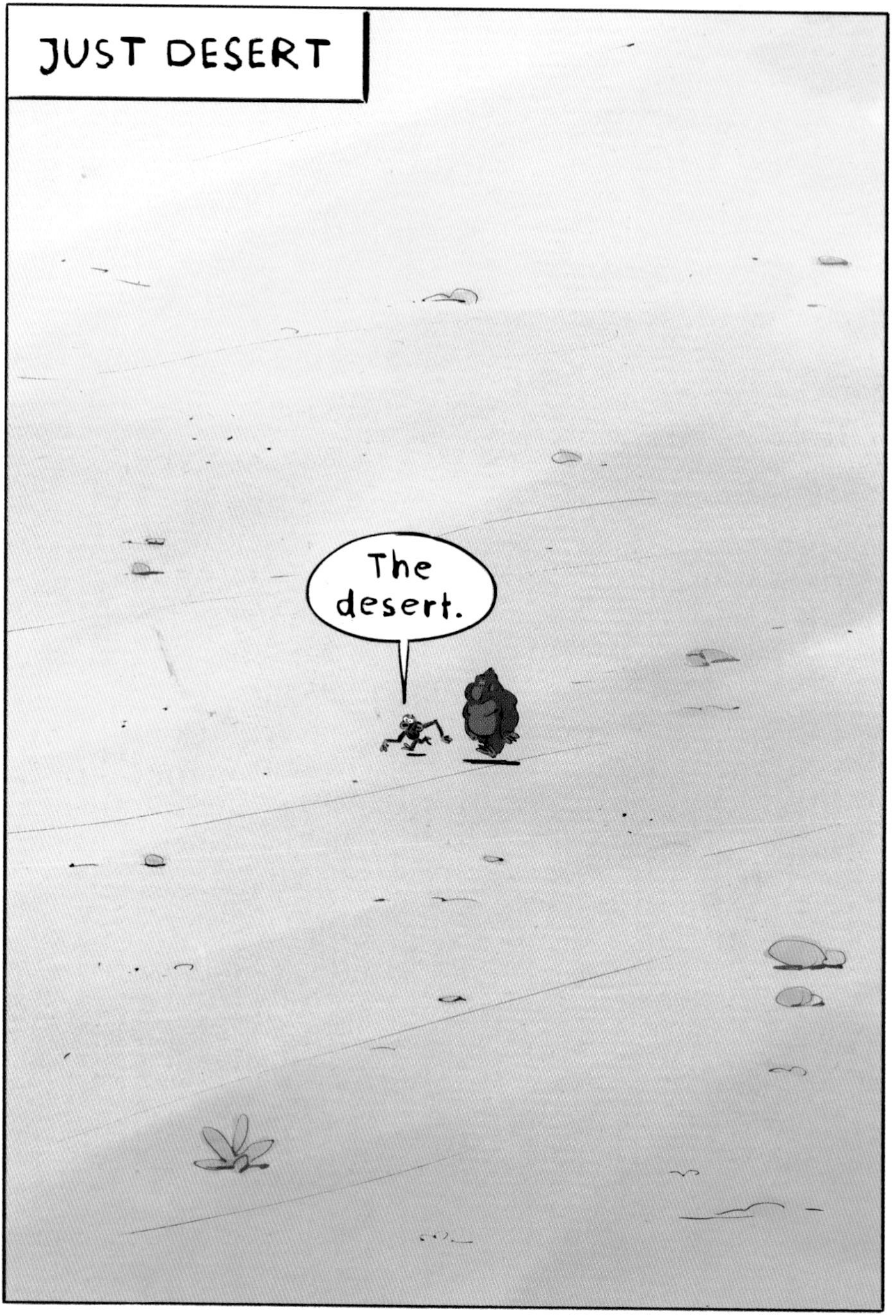
JUST DESERT
The desert.

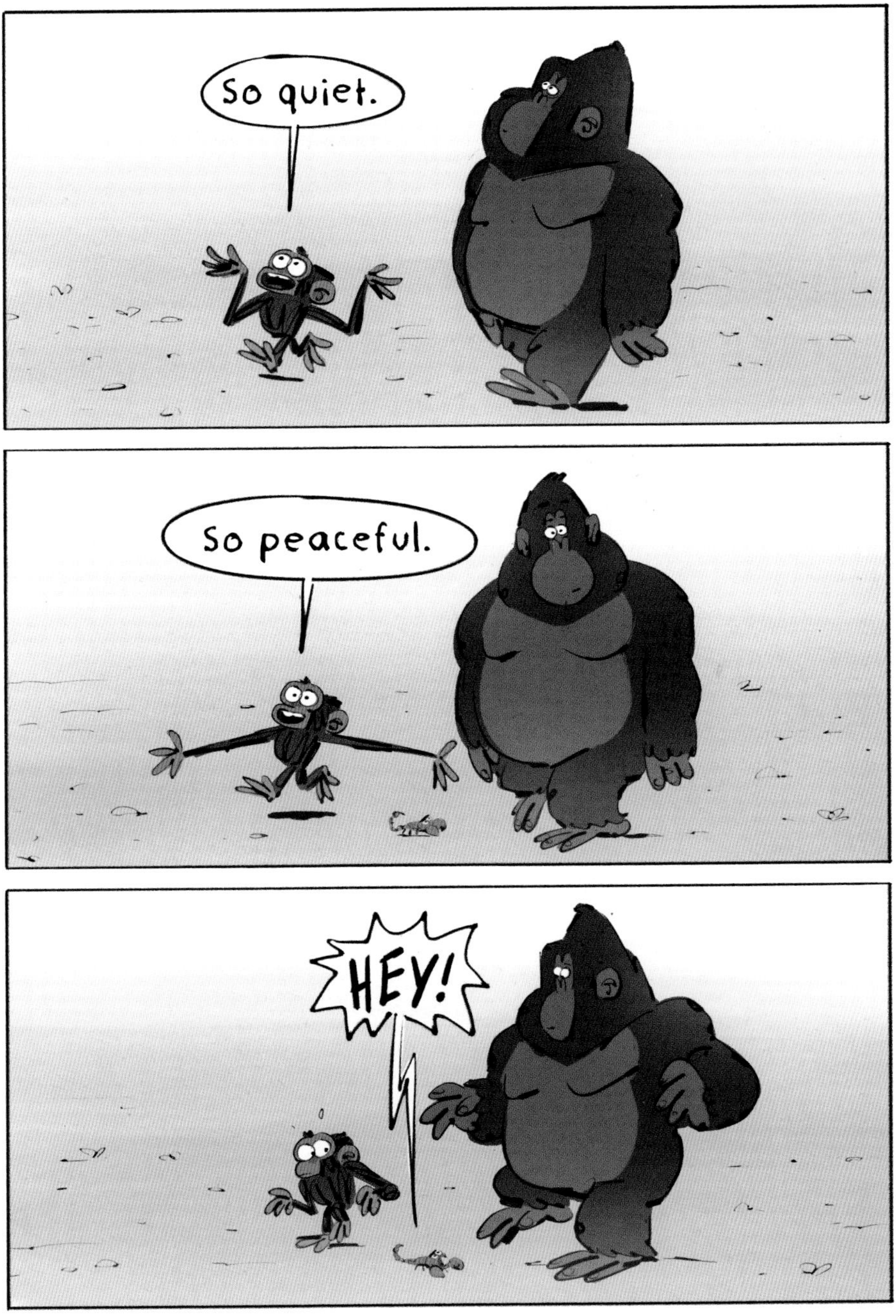
So quiet.
So peaceful.
HEY!

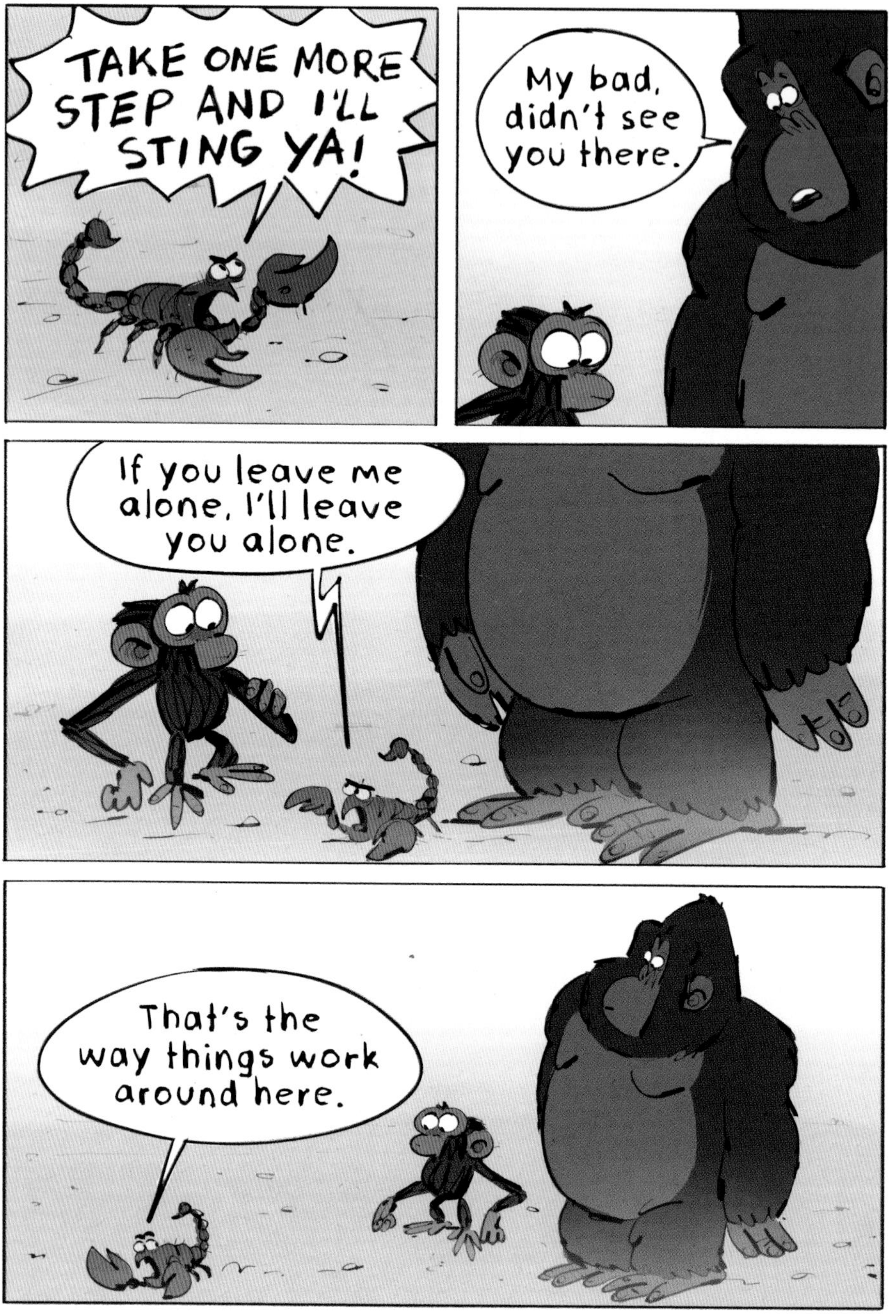
TAKE ONE MORE STEP AND I'LL STING YA!
My bad, didn't see you there.
If you leave me alone, I'll leave you alone.
That's the way things work around here.

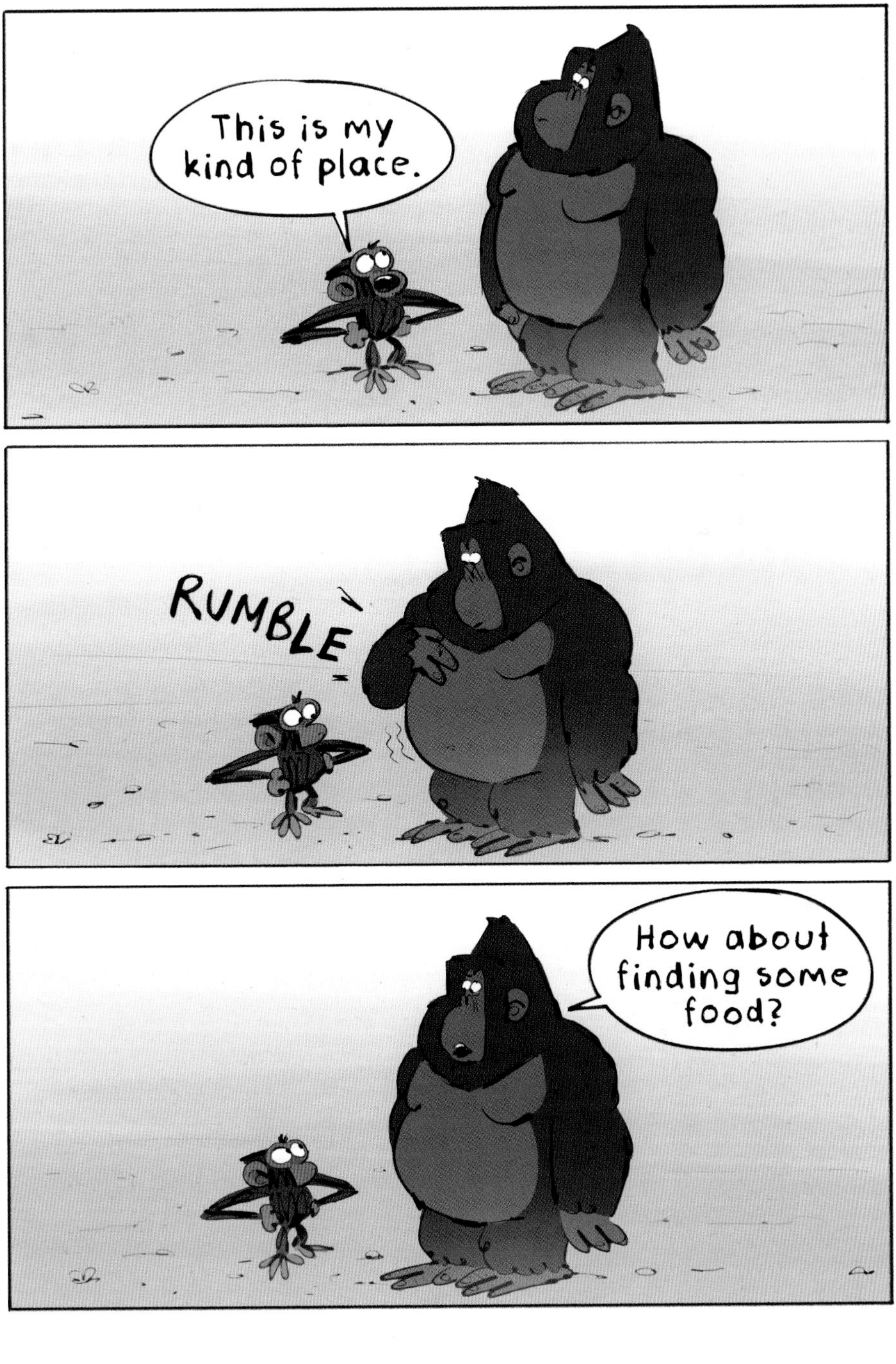
This is my kind of place.
RUMBLE
How about finding some food?

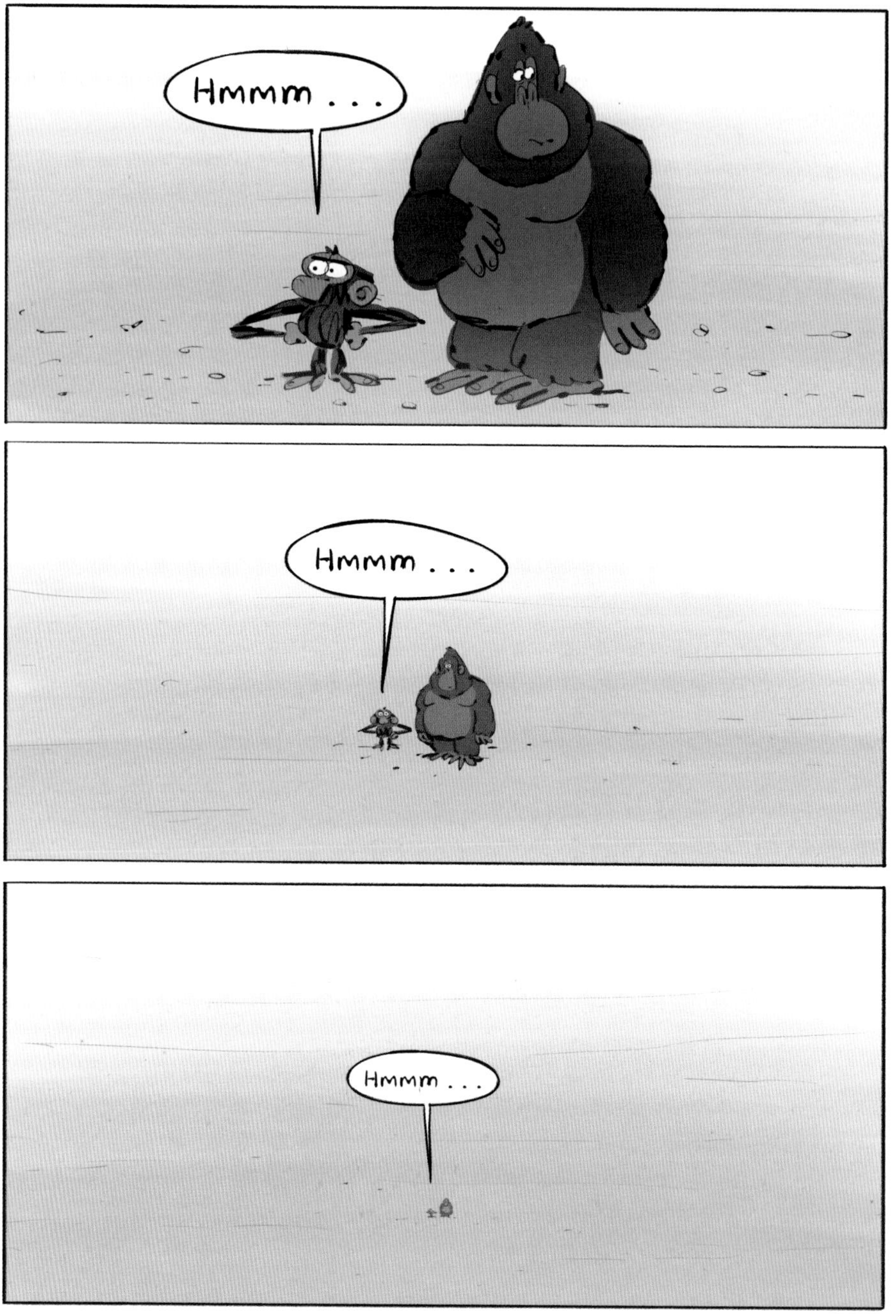
Hmmm . . .
Hmmm . . .
Hmmm . . .

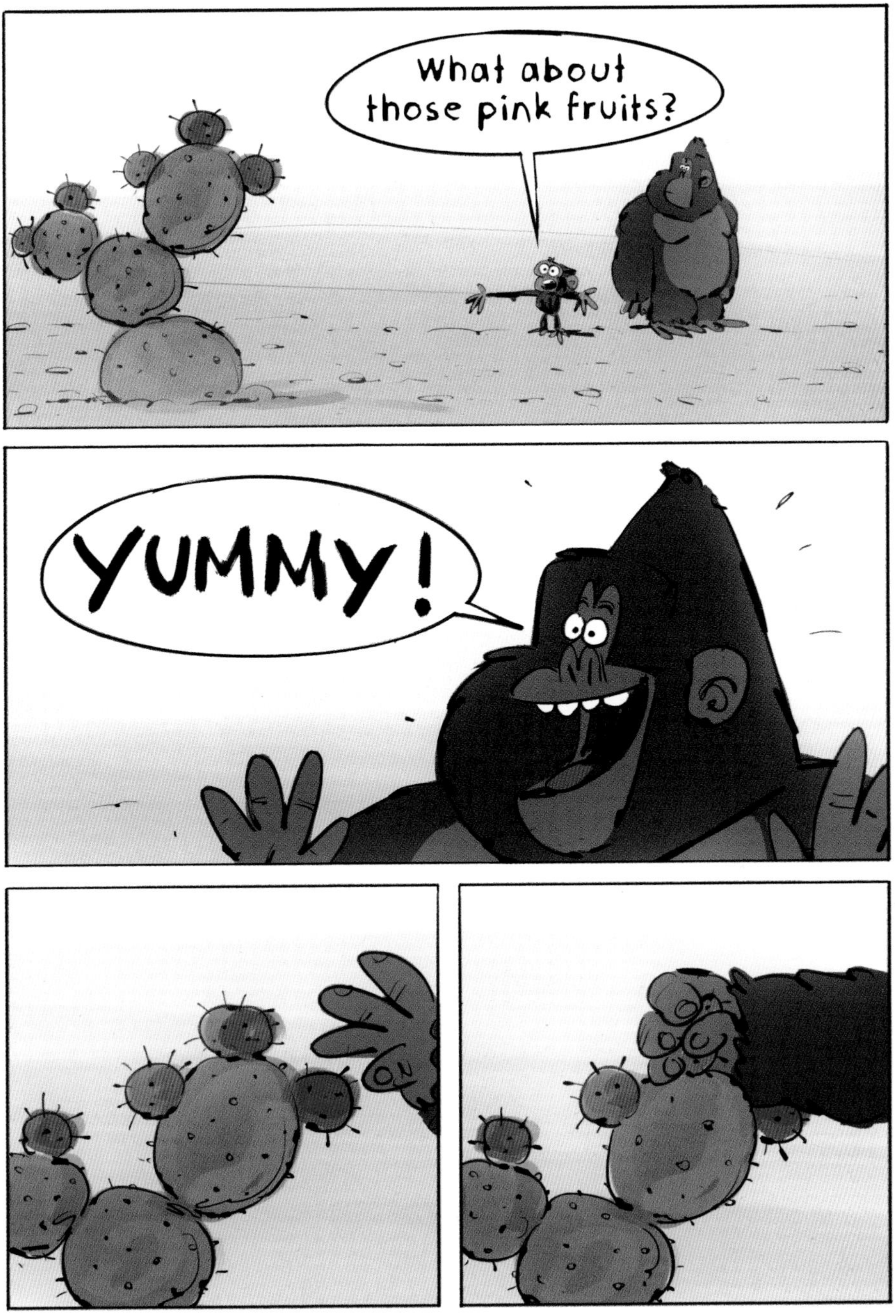
What about those pink fruits?
YUMMY!

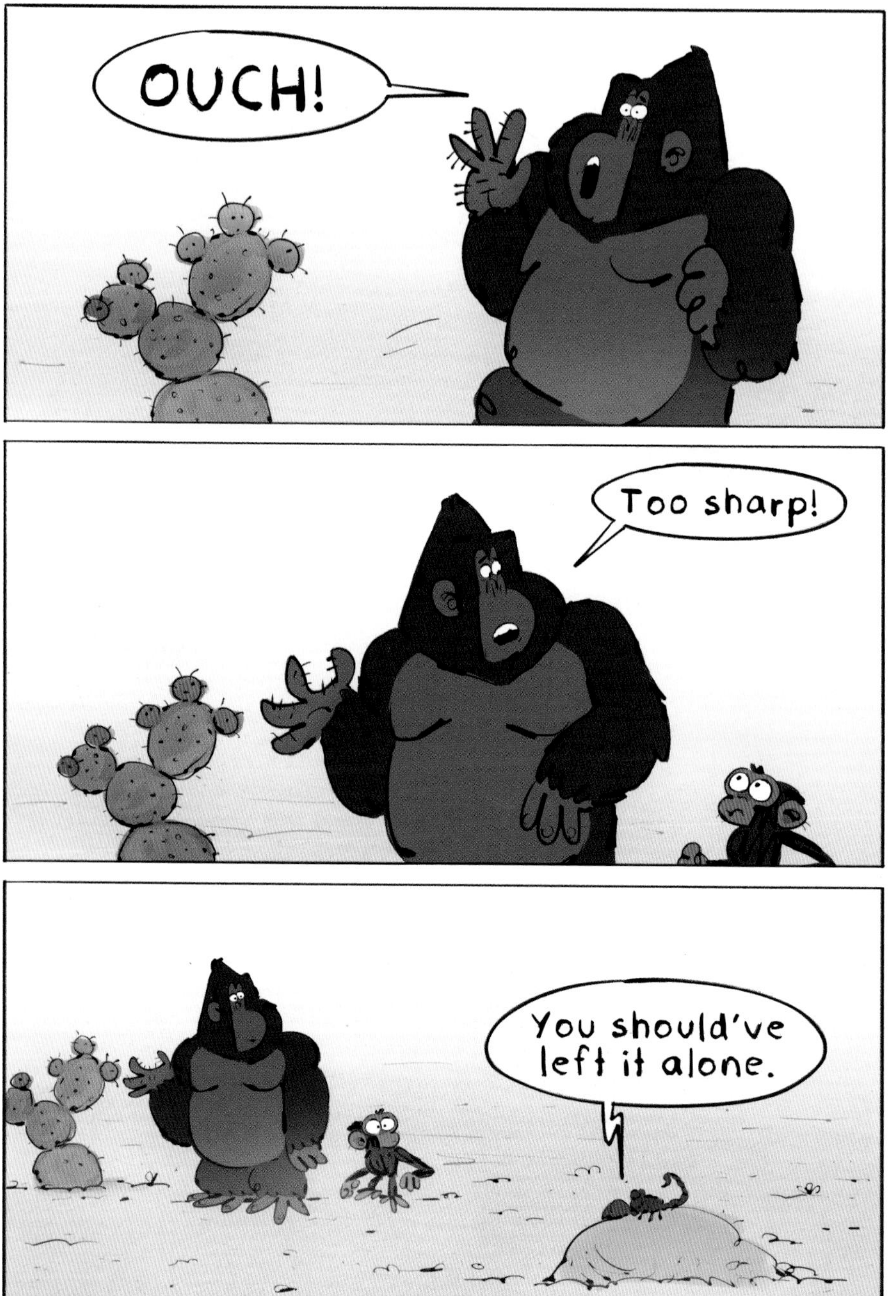
OUCH!
Too sharp!
You should've left it alone.

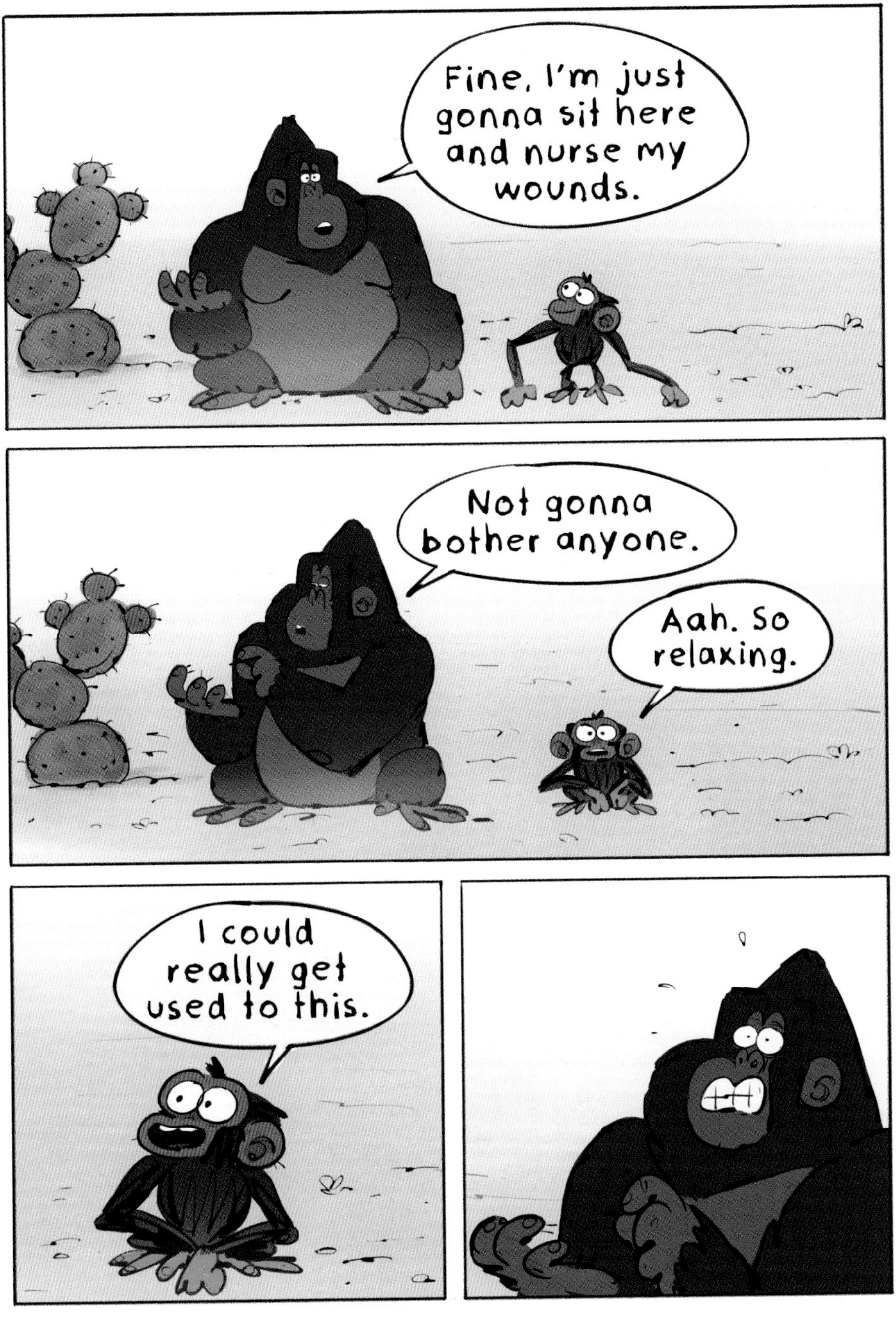
Fine, I'm just gonna sit here and nurse my wounds.
Not gonna bother anyone.
Aah. So relaxing.
I could really get used to this.

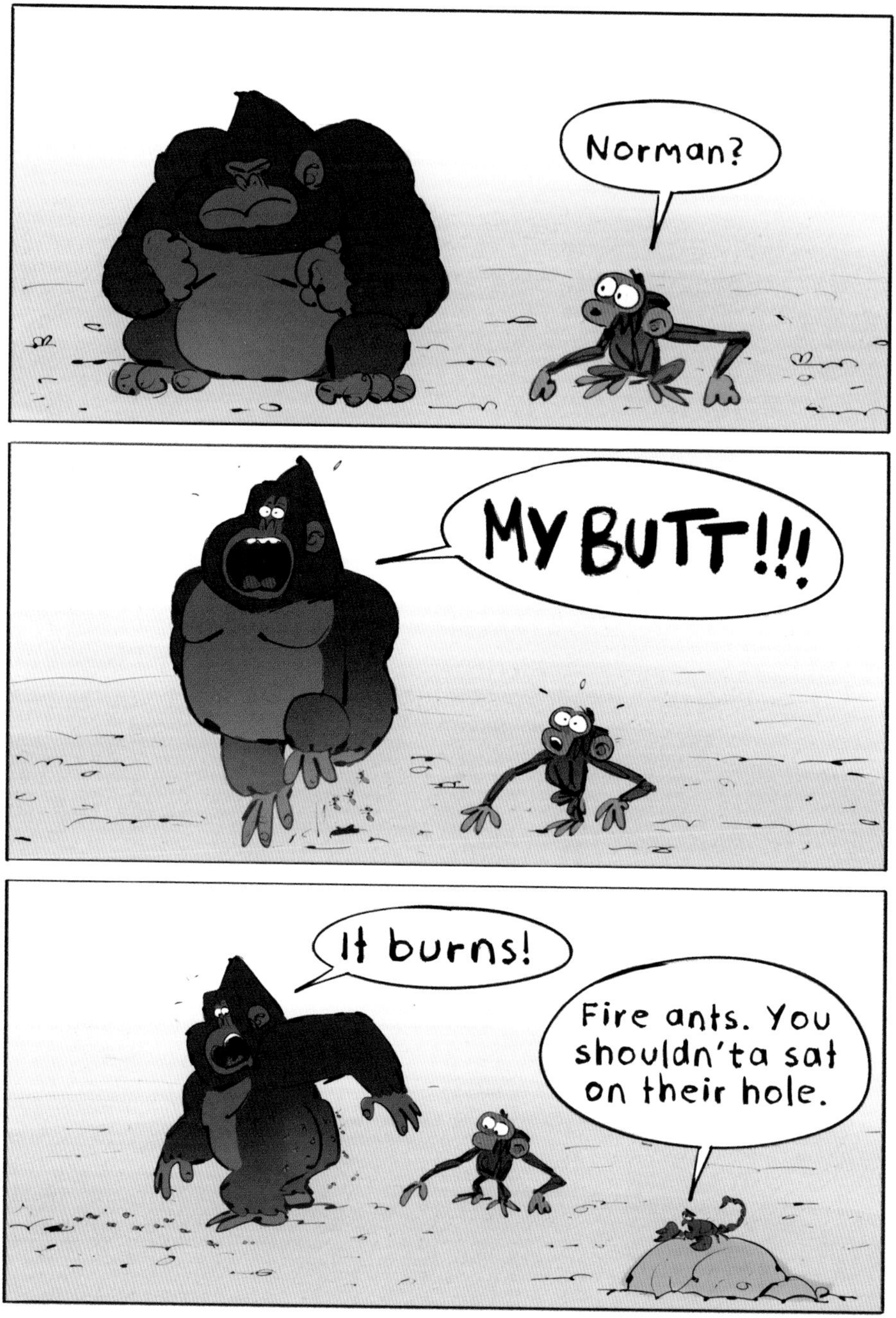

Norman?
MY BUTT!!!
It burns!
Fire ants. You shouldn'ta sat on their hole.

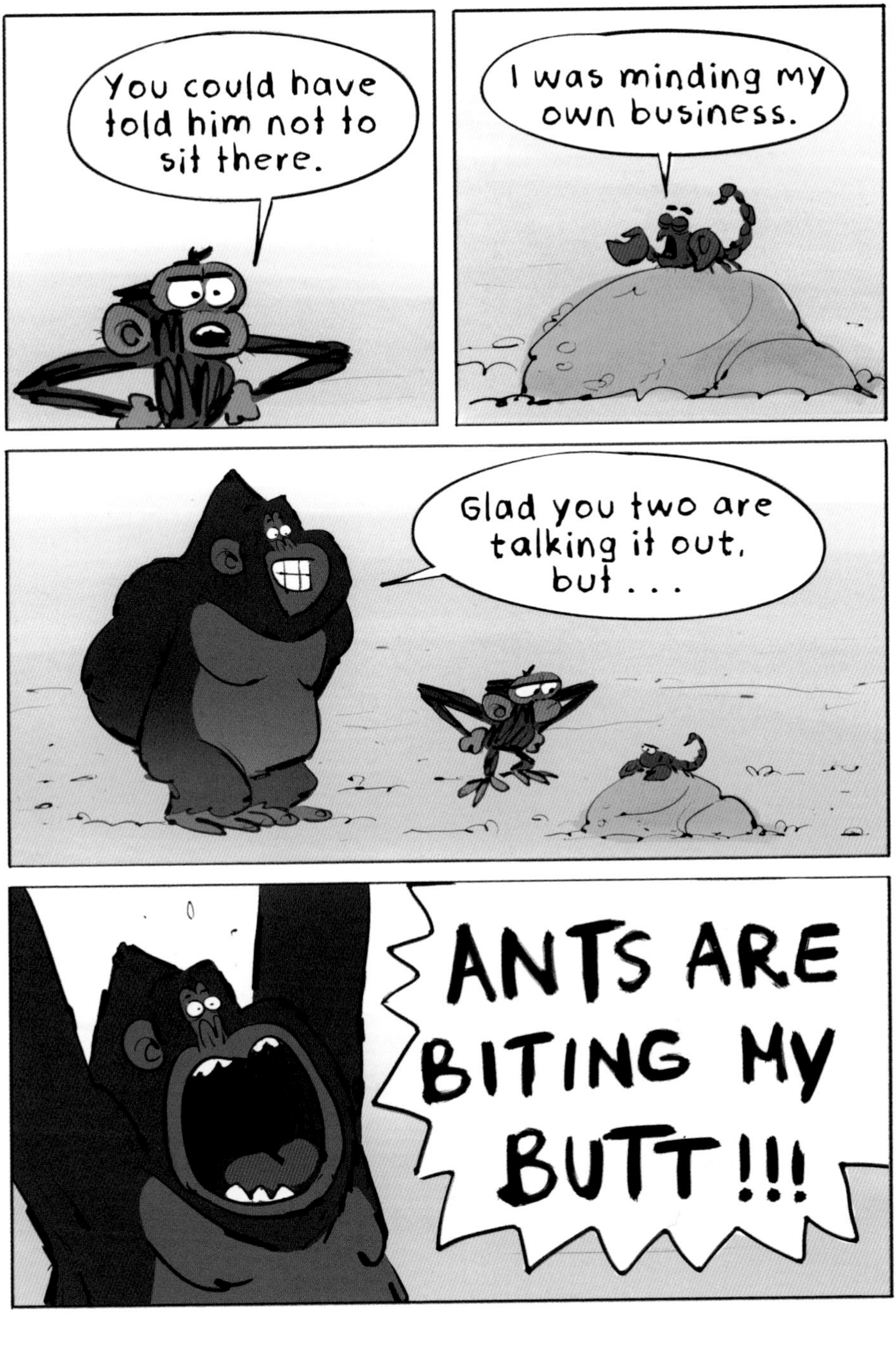
You could have told him not to sit there.
I was minding my own business.
Glad you two are talking it out, but . . .
ANTS ARE BITING MY BUTT!!!

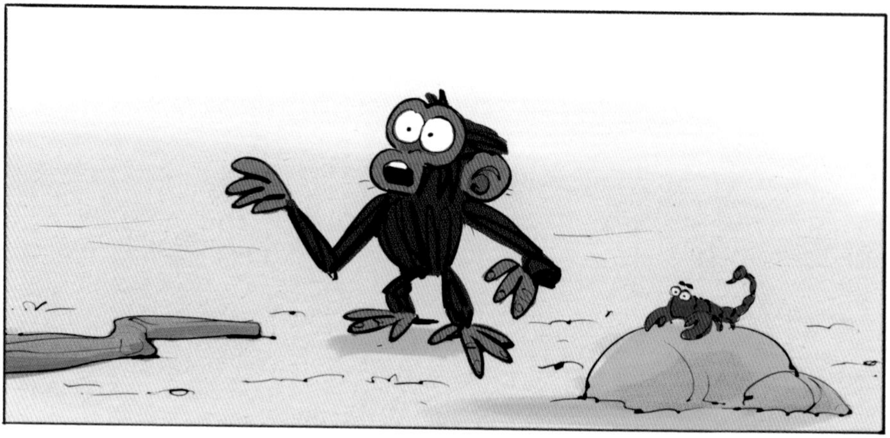

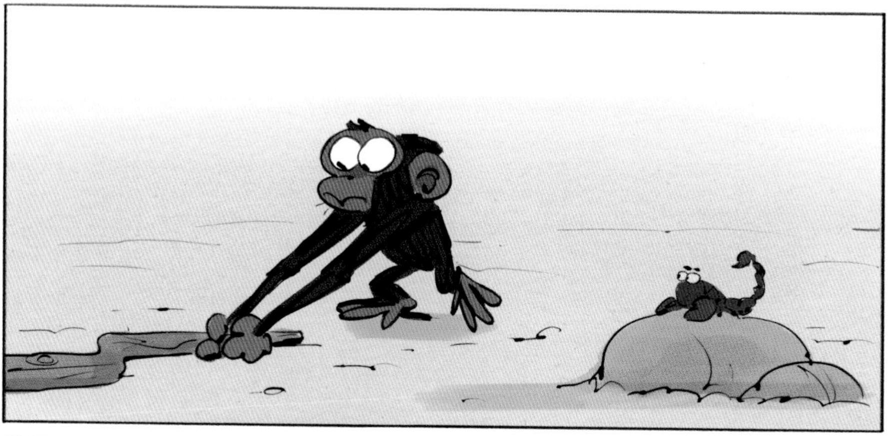

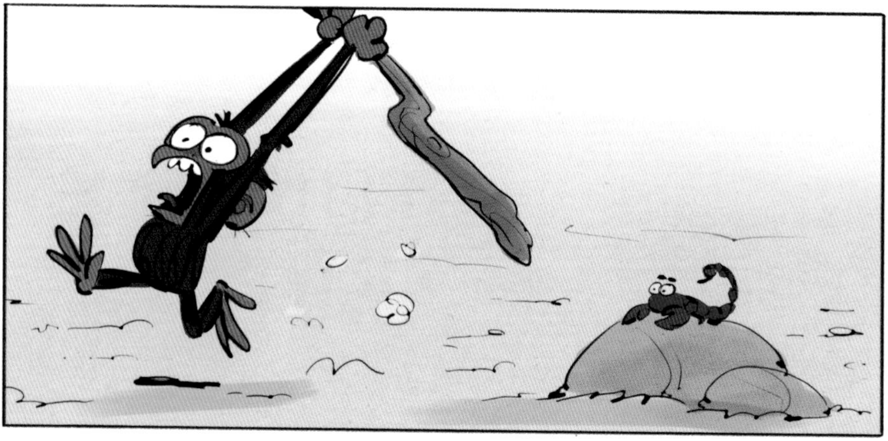

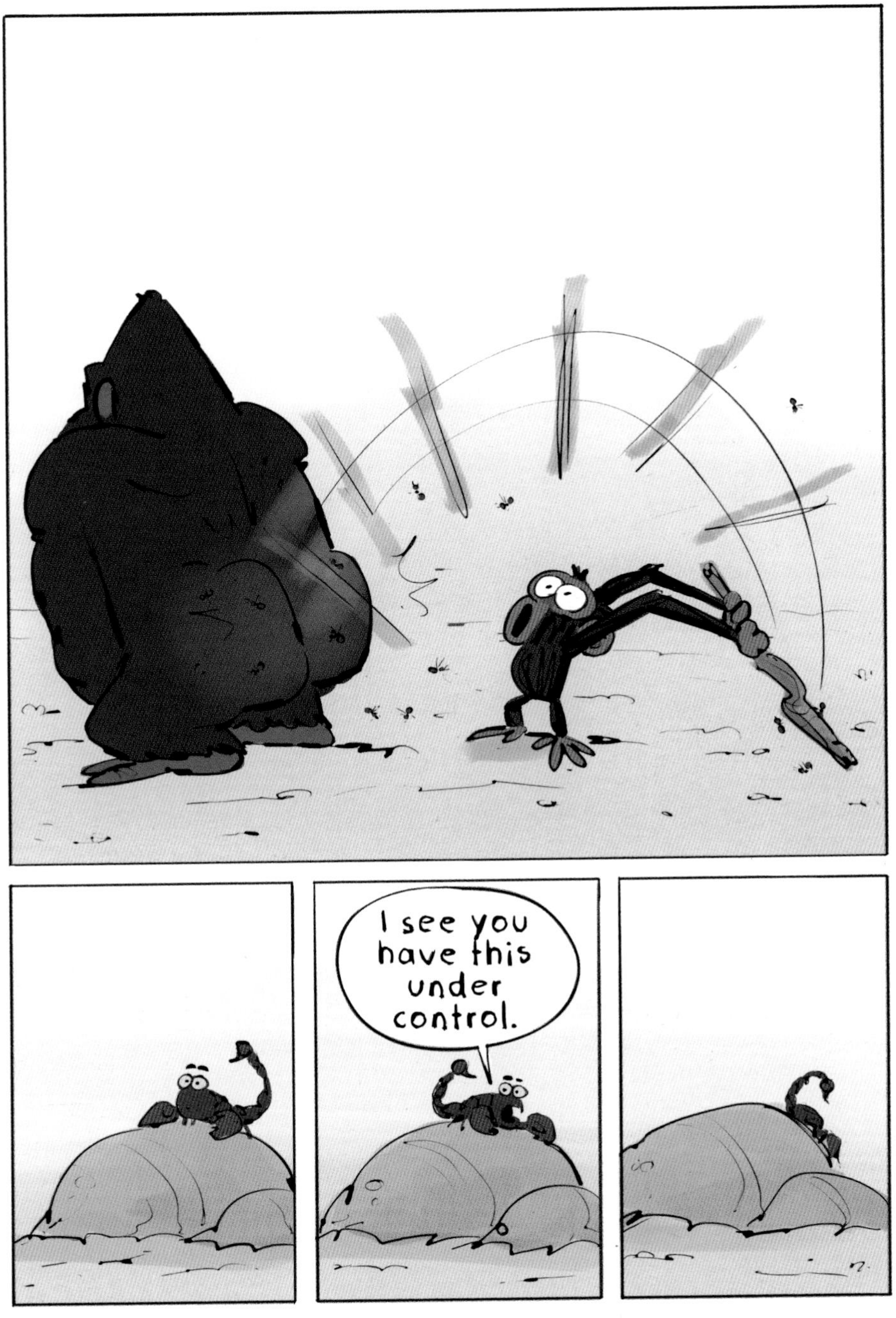
I see you have this under control.

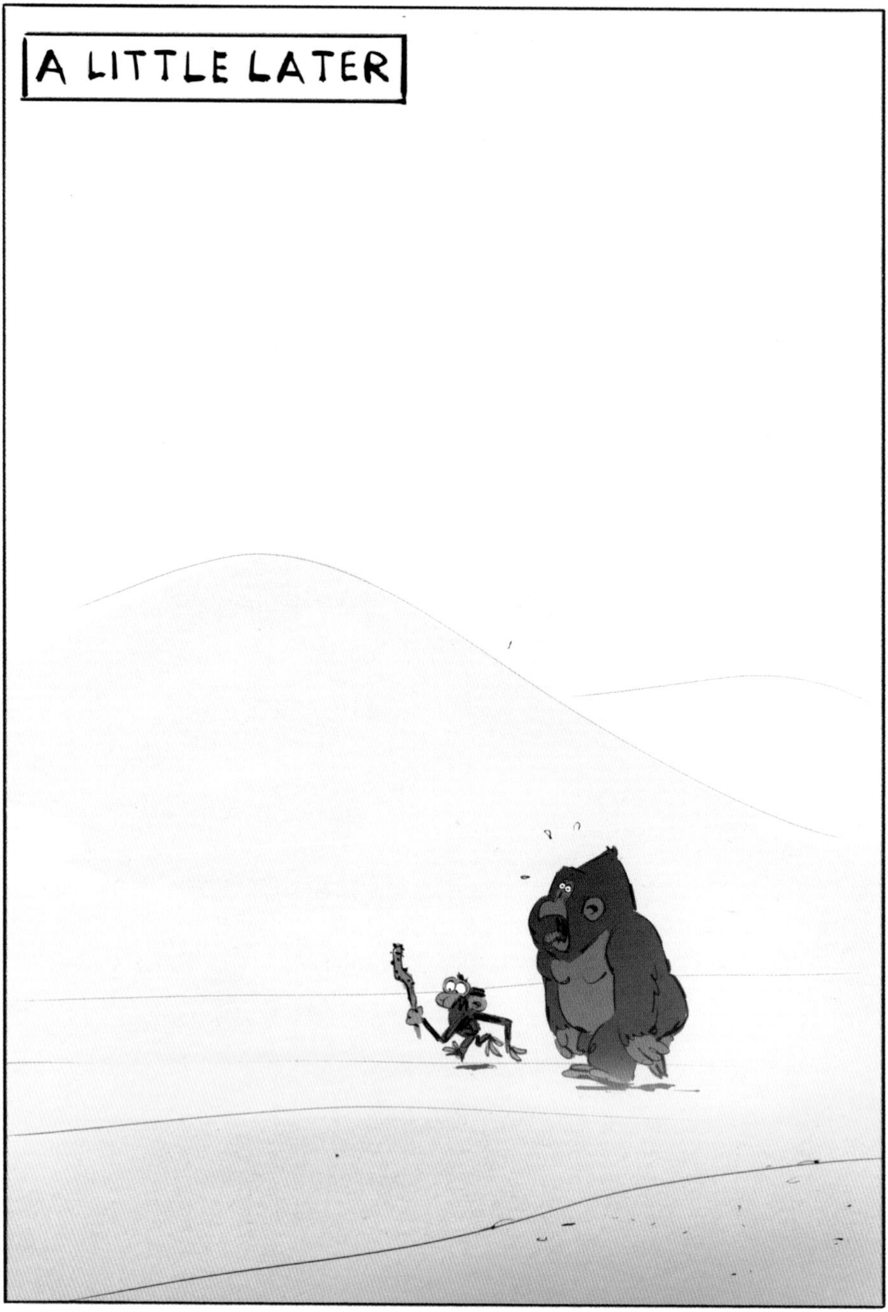
A LITTLE LATER

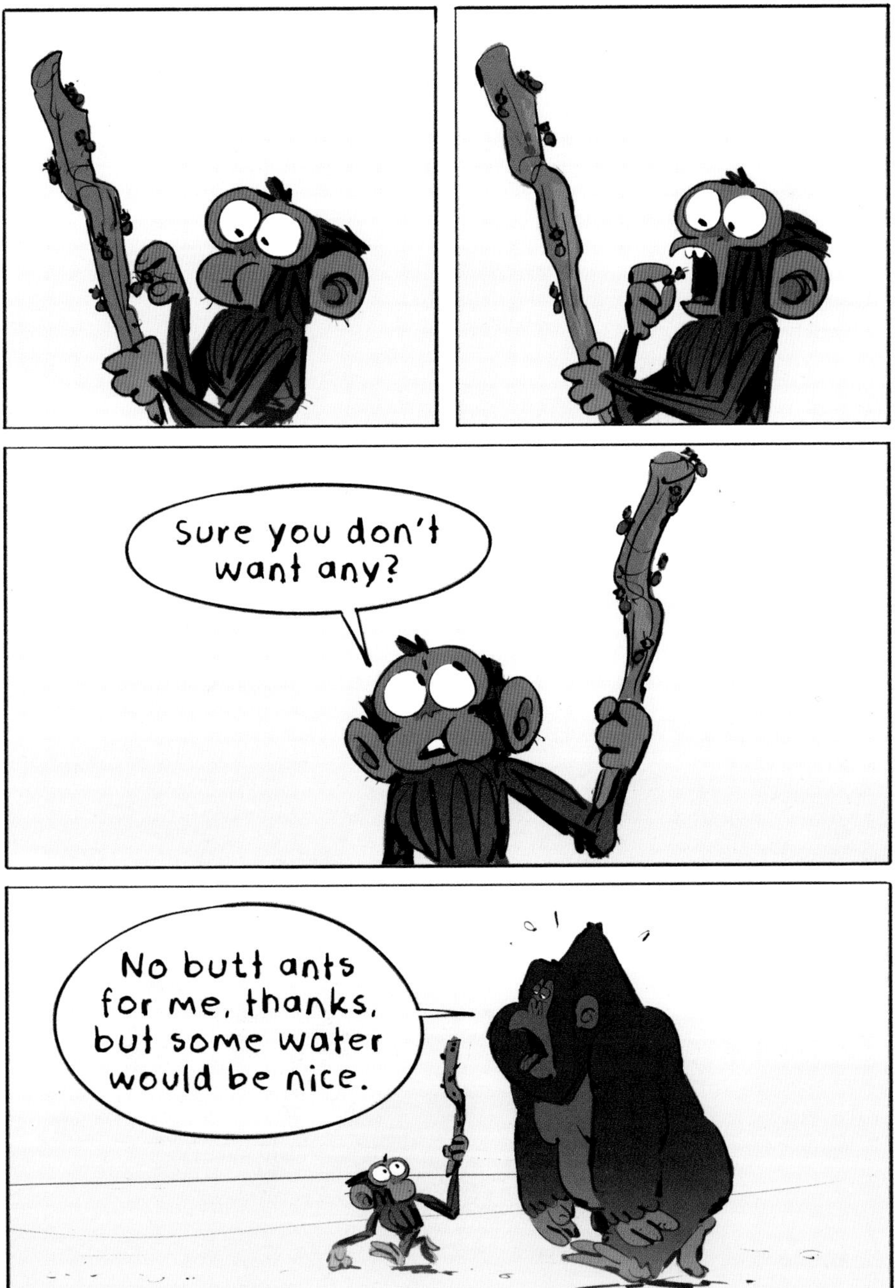
Sure you don't want any?
No butt ants for me, thanks, but some water would be nice.

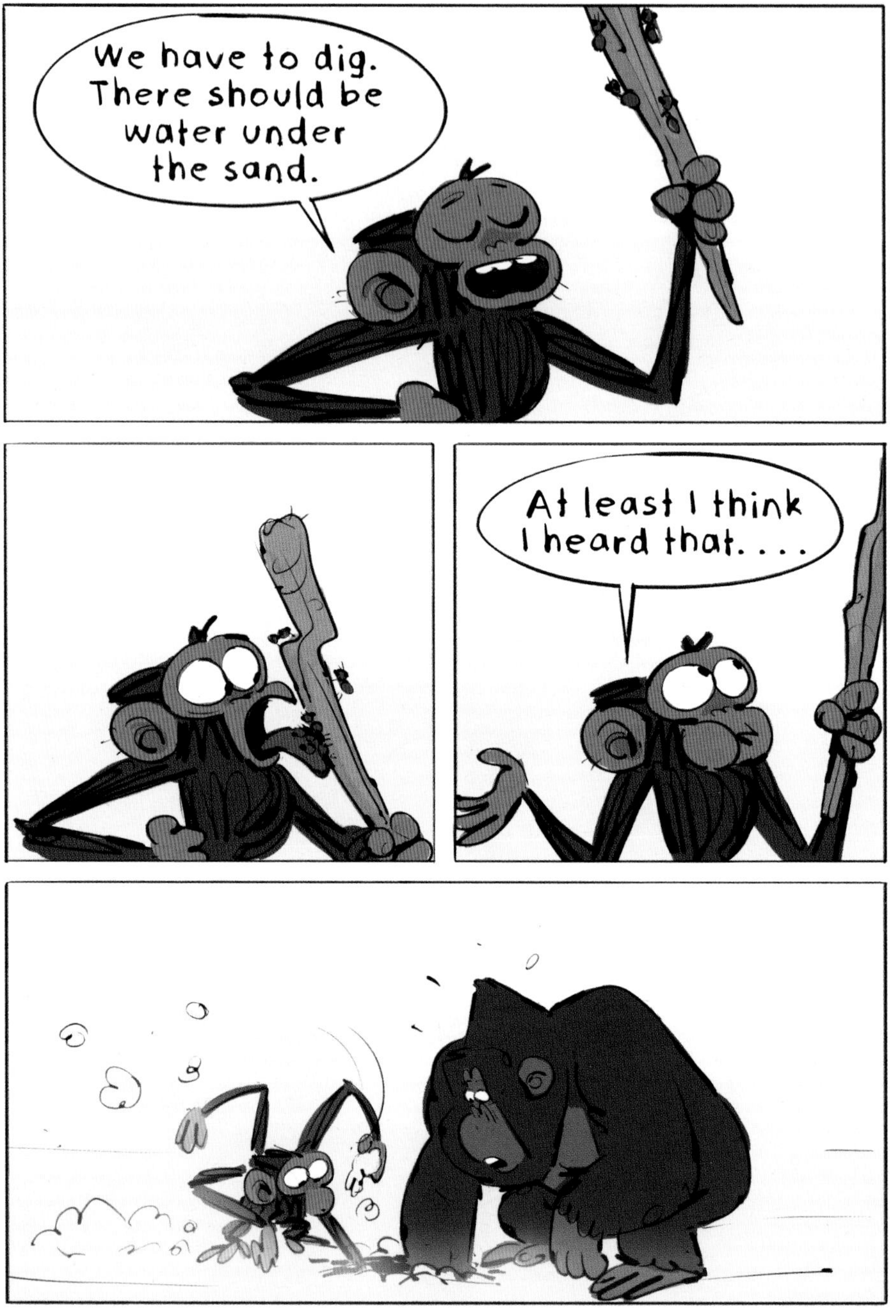
We have to dig. There should be water under the sand.
At least I think I heard that. . . .

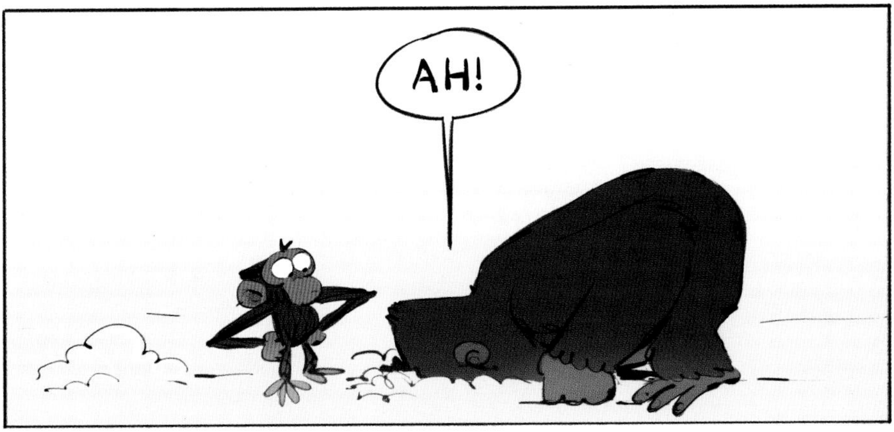
AH!

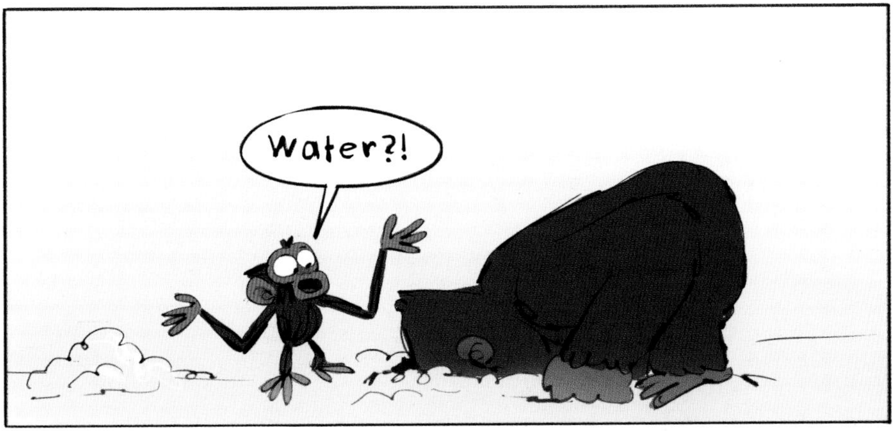
Water?!

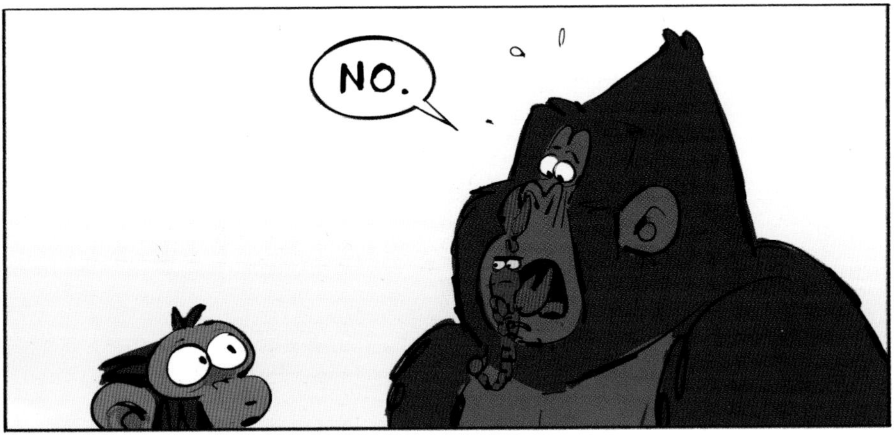
NO.

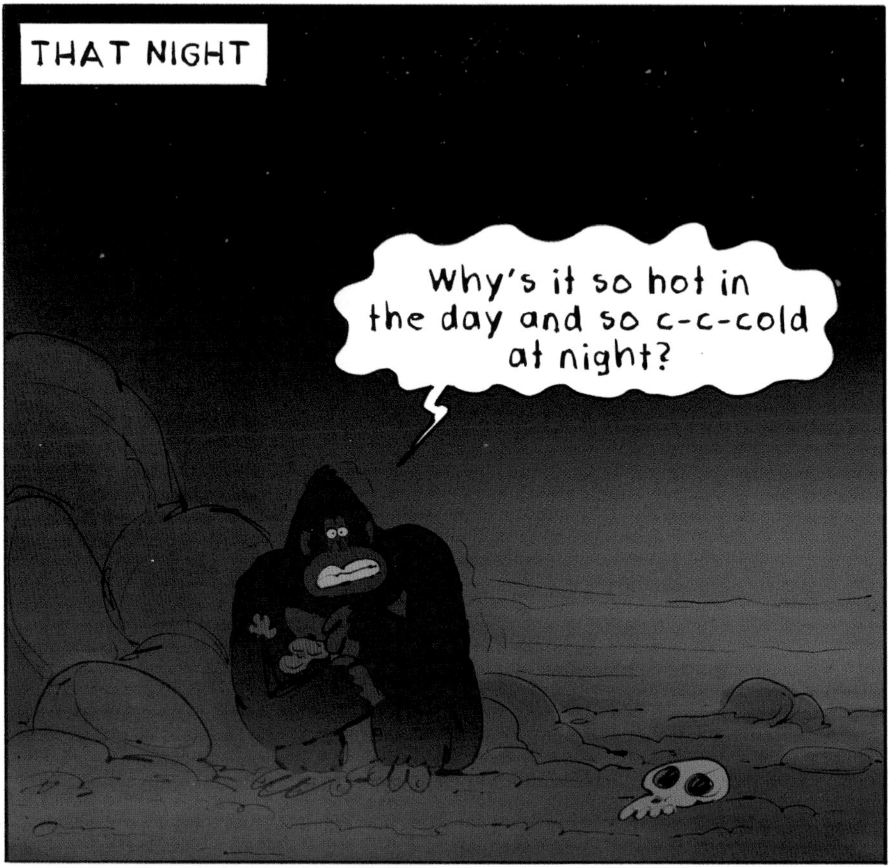
THAT NIGHT
Why's it so hot in the day and so c-c-cold at night?
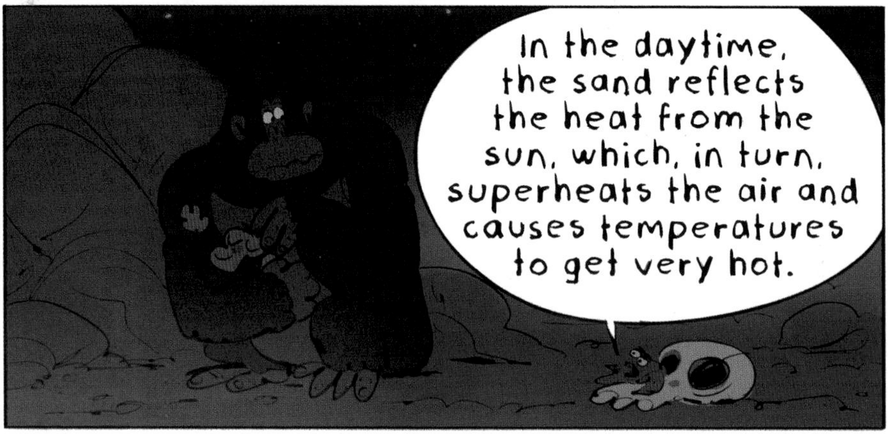
In the daytime, the sand reflects the heat from the sun, which, in turn, superheats the air and causes temperatures to get very hot.

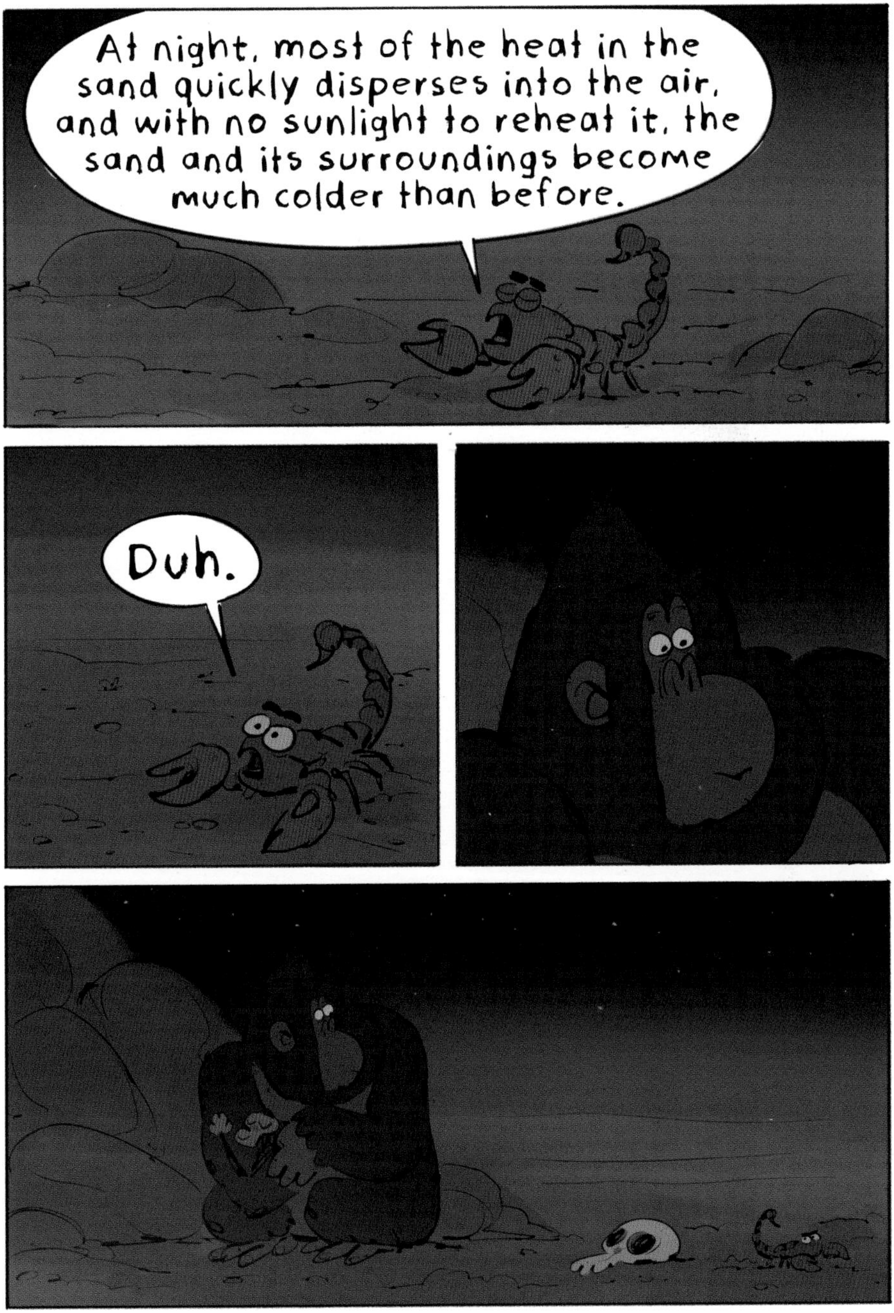
At night, most of the heat in the sand quickly disperses into the air, and with no sunlight to reheat it, the sand and its surroundings become much colder than before.
Duh.

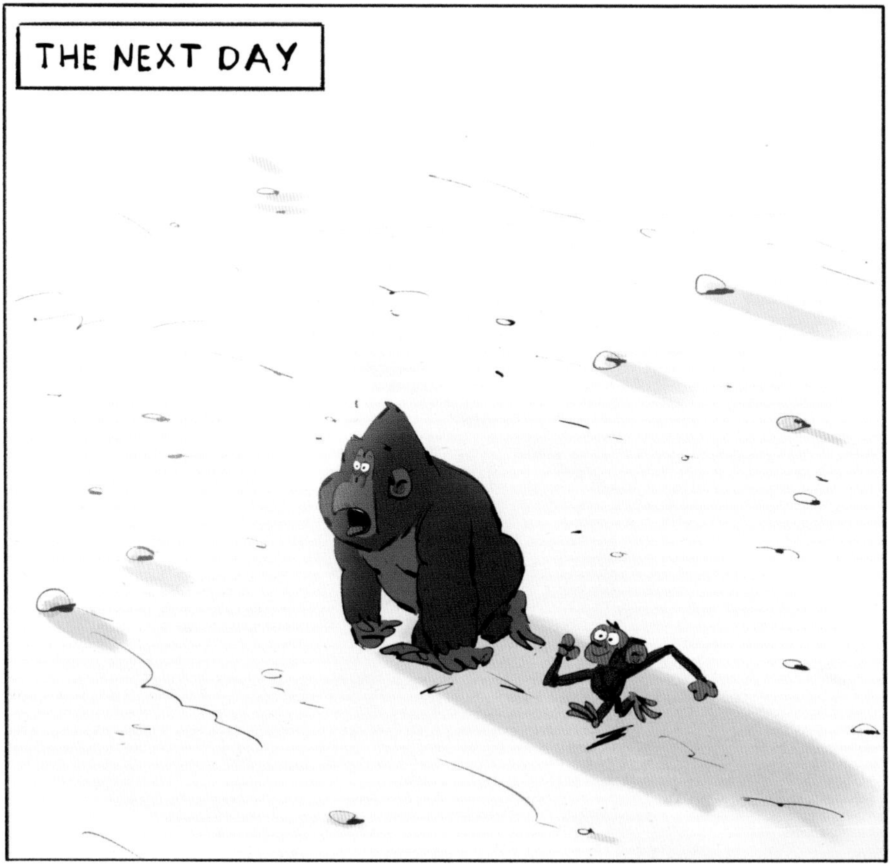
THE NEXT DAY

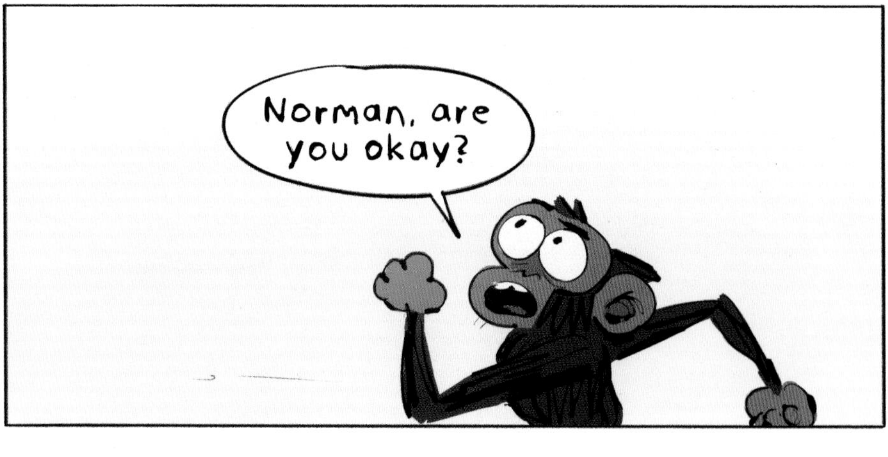
Norman, are you okay?

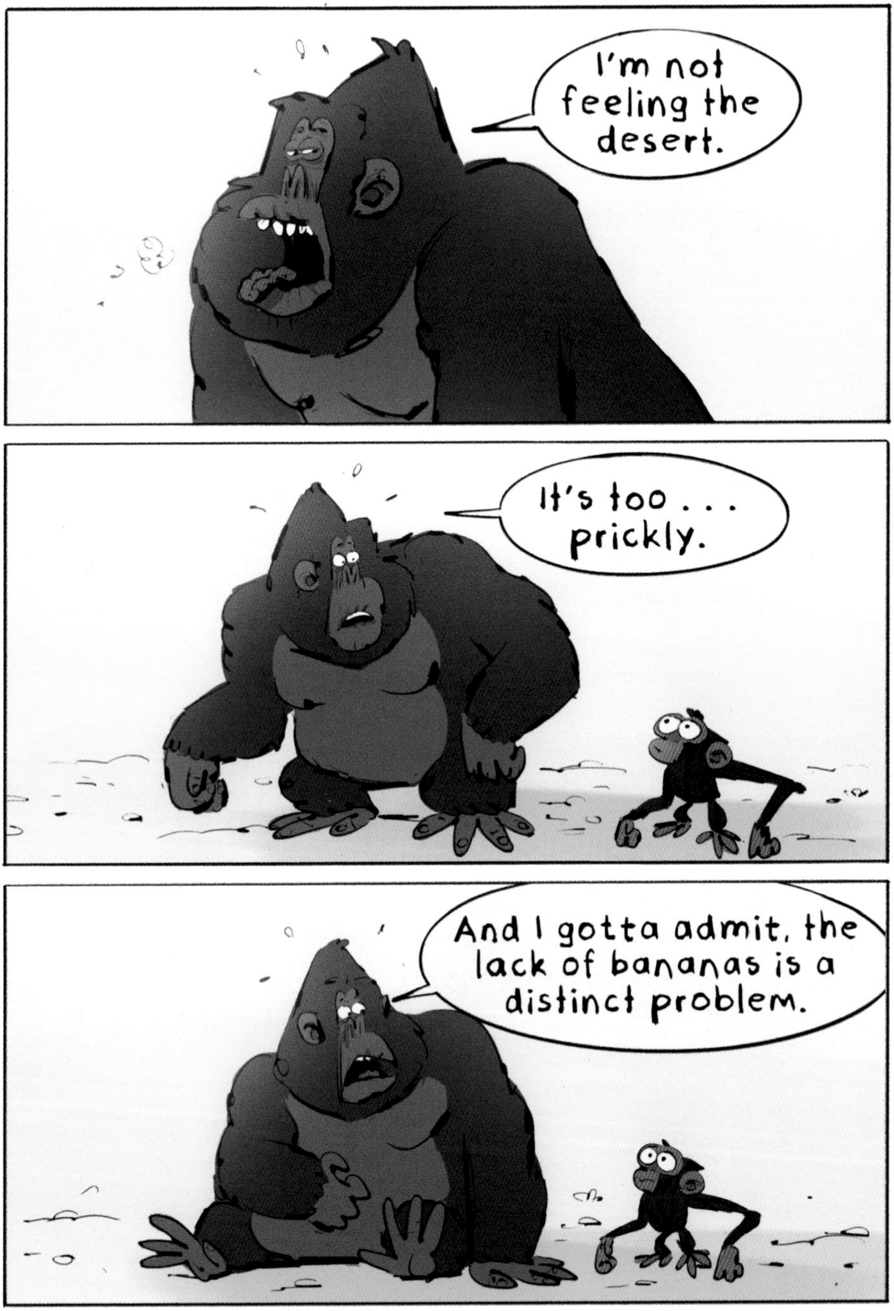
I'm not feeling the desert.
It's too . . . prickly.
And I gotta admit, the lack of bananas is a distinct problem.

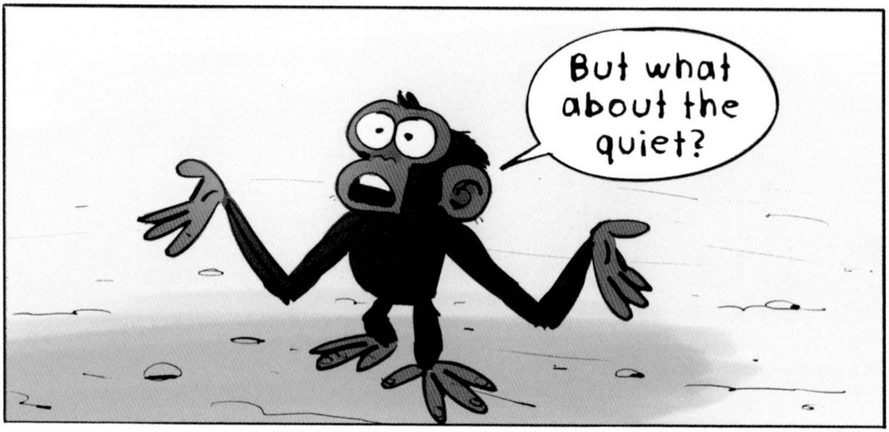
But what about the quiet?

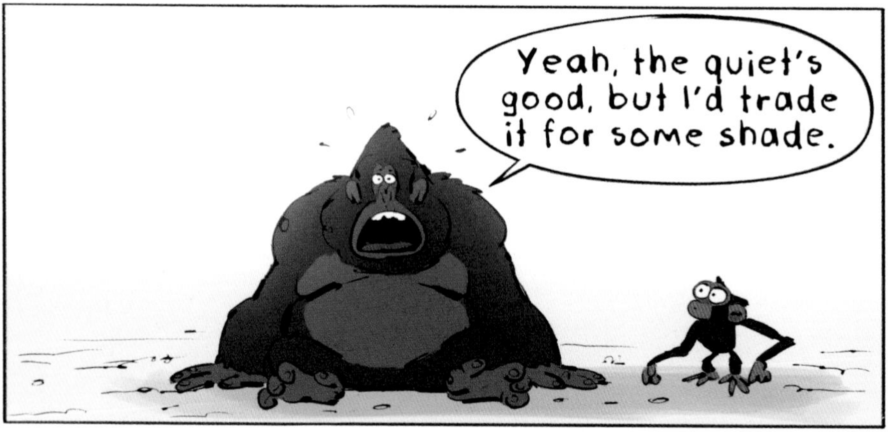
Yeah, the quiet's good, but I'd trade it for some shade.

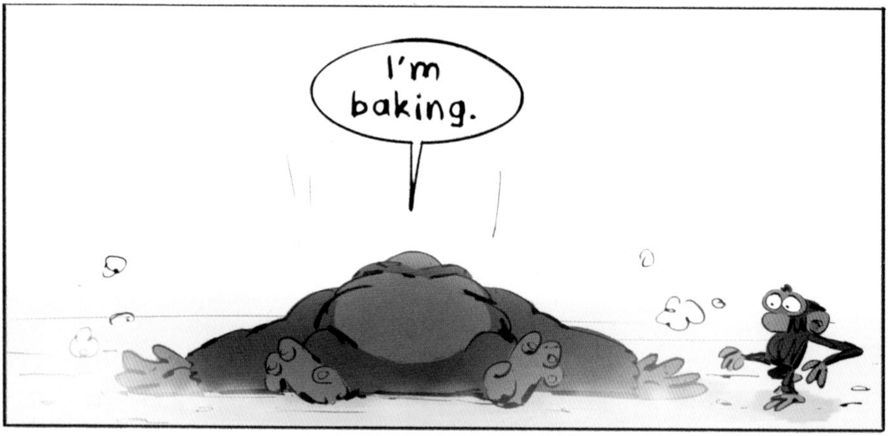
I'm baking.

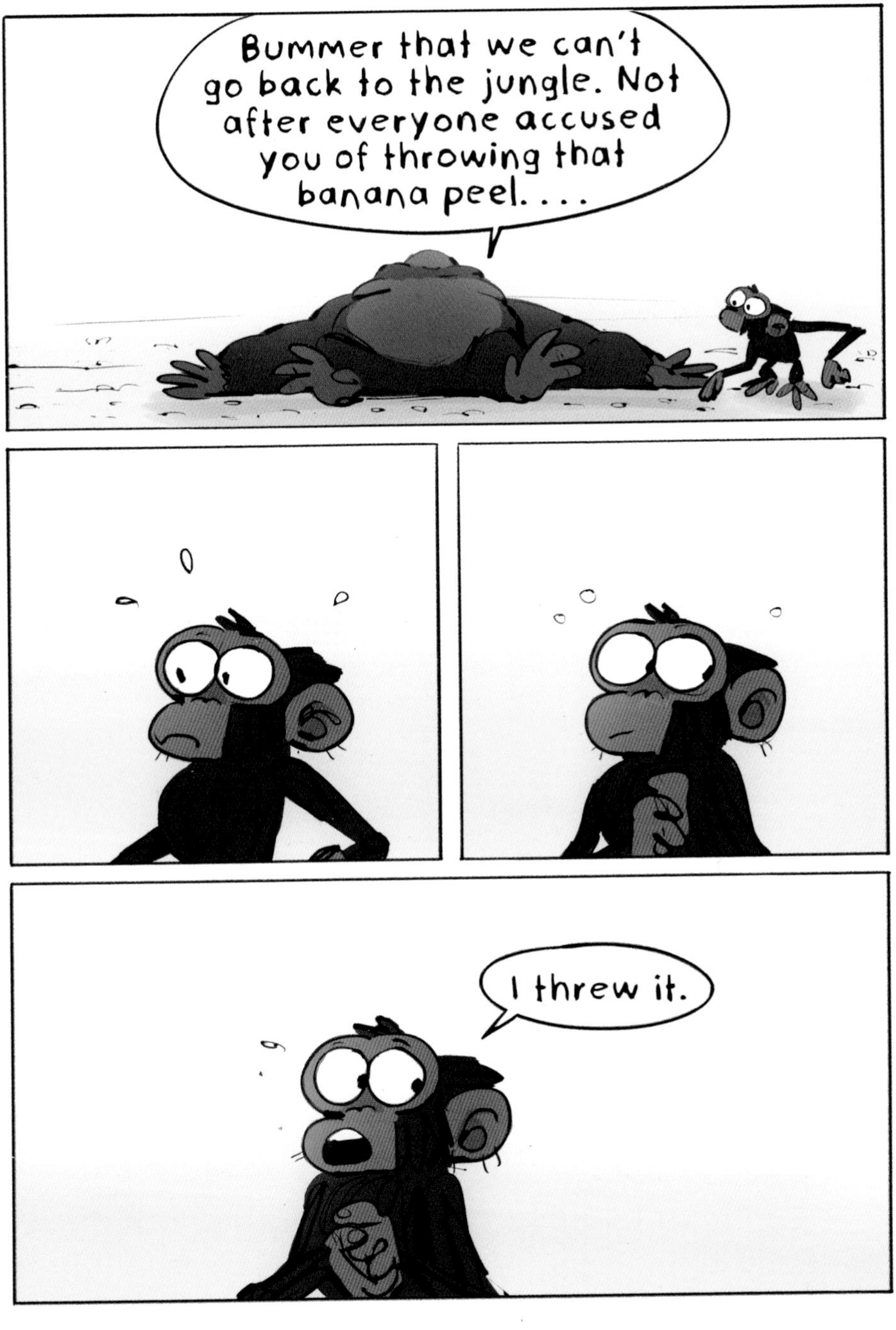
Bummer that we can't go back to the jungle. Not after everyone accused you of throwing that banana peel. . . .
I threw it.

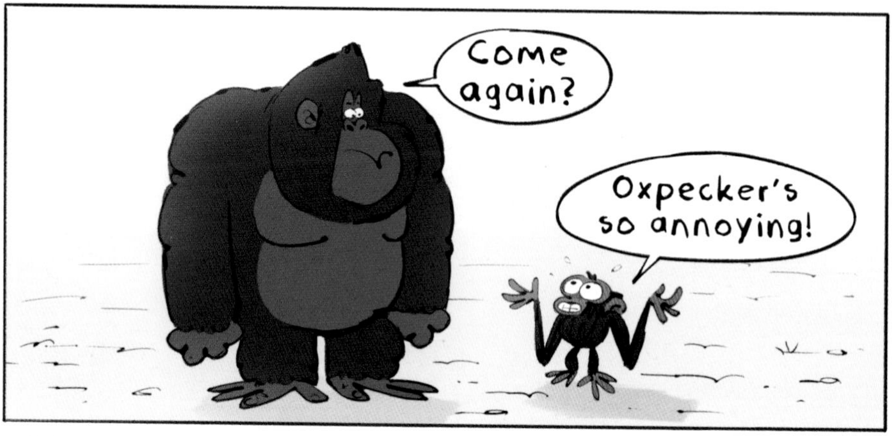
Come again?
Oxpecker's so annoying!

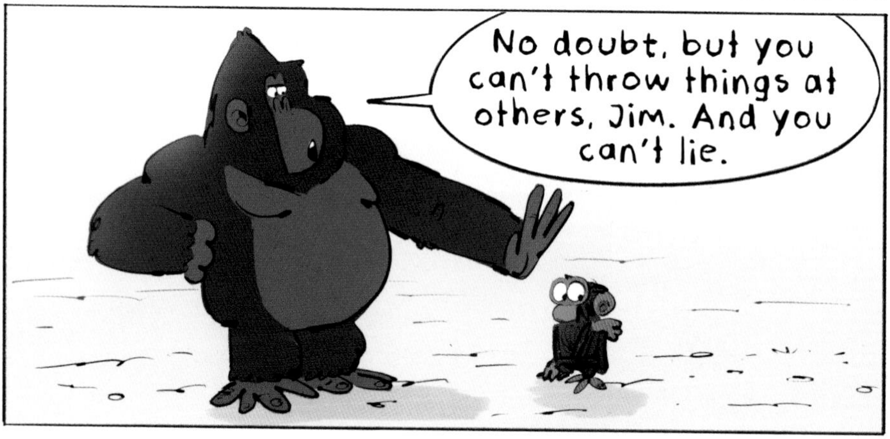
No doubt, but you can't throw things at others, Jim. And you can't lie.

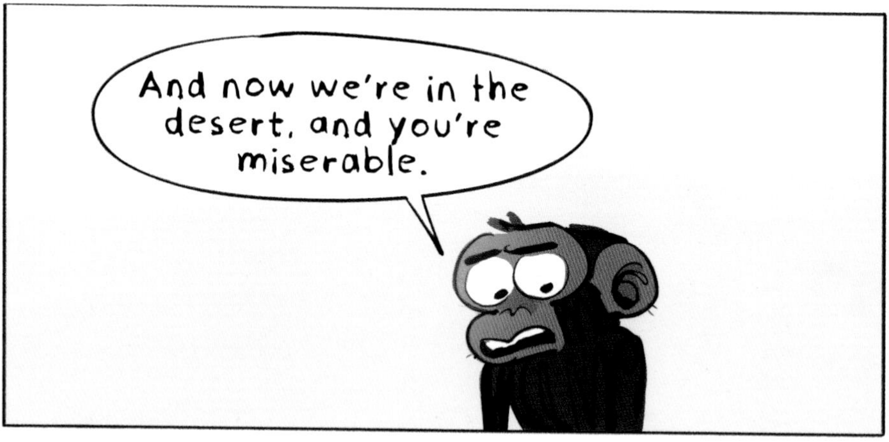
And now we're in the desert, and you're miserable.

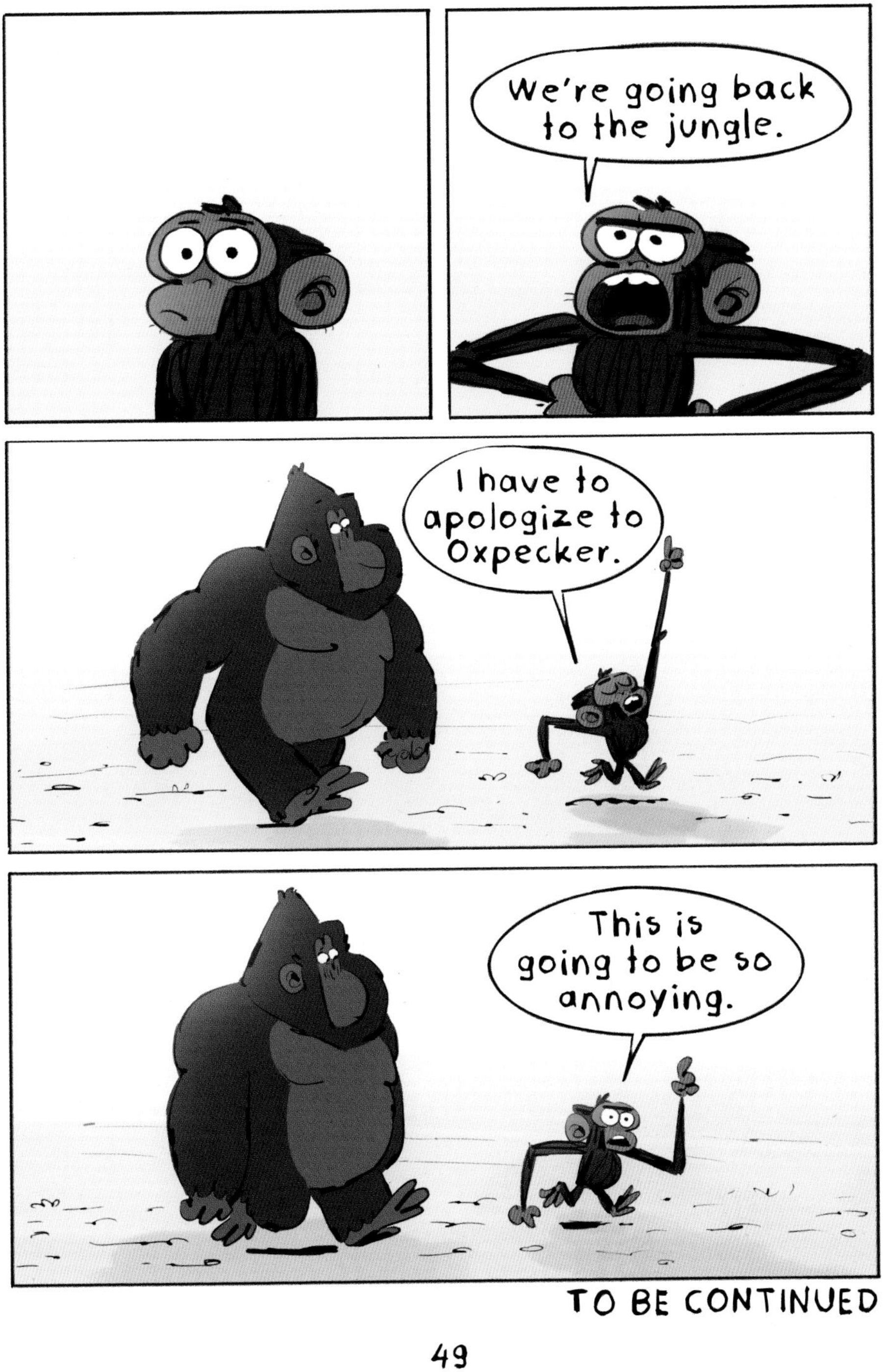
We're going back to the jungle.
I have to apologize to Oxpecker.
This is going to be so annoying.

TO BE CONTINUED

CHOMP & CHAT WITH CHIP PANZEE

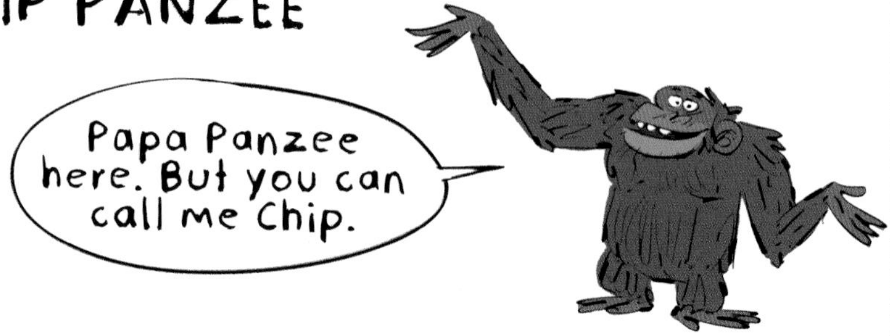
Papa Panzee here. But you can call me Chip.

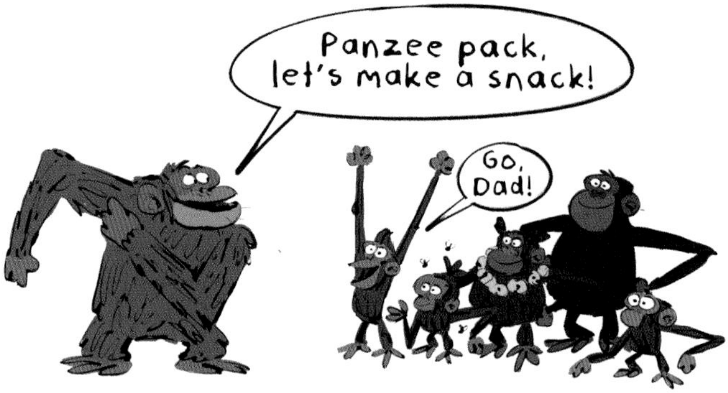
Panzee pack, let's make a snack!
Go, Dad!

Today's snack:
CHIP'S CHIMP CHOMPERS

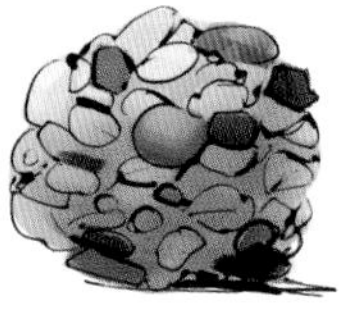

YOU'LL NEED:
Large mixing bowl
Big spoon
Tablespoon, cookie scoop,
  or ice cream scoop
Baking sheet

INGREDIENTS:

- 1 cup rolled oats
- 1/2 cup chocolate chips
- 1/4 cup raisins
- 1/4 cup candy-coated chocolate drops (such as M&Ms)
- 3/4 cup peanut butter (or any nut butter you like)
- 1 tbsp. honey
- Pinch of salt
- 1/4 cup chopped nuts (whatever kind you like)

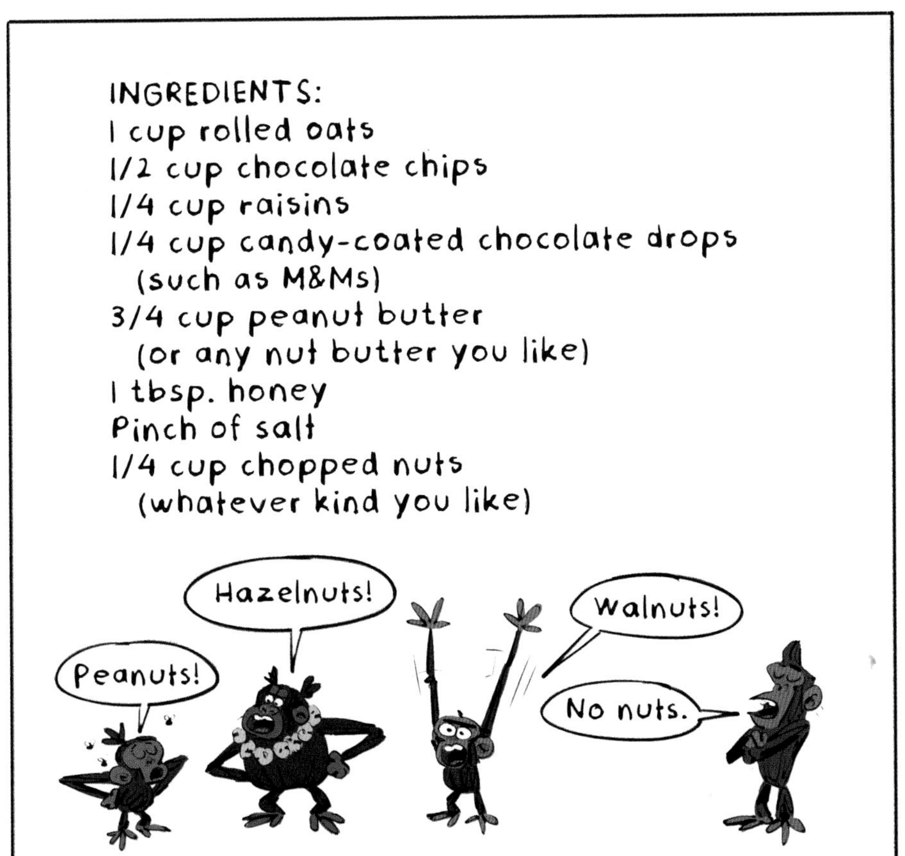
Peanuts!
Hazelnuts!
Walnuts!
No nuts.

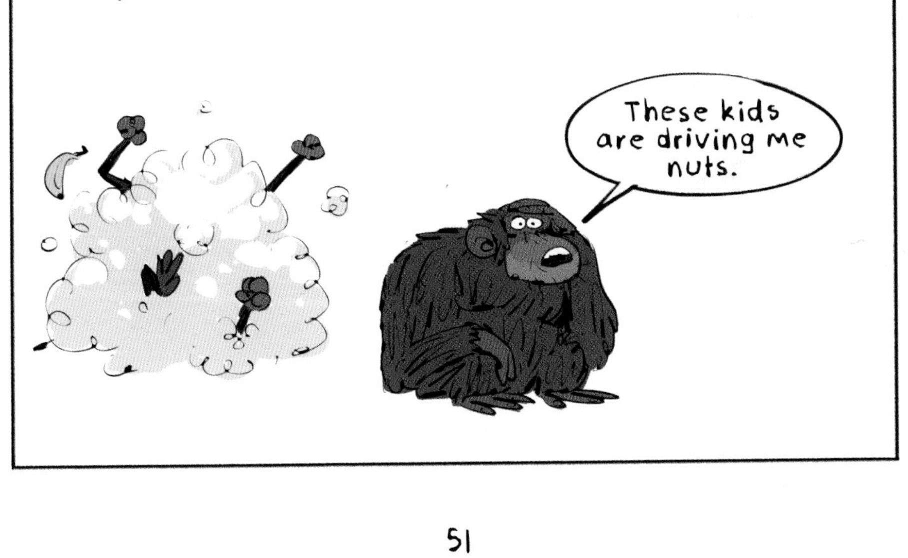
These kids are driving me nuts.

INSTRUCTIONS

1. Put all the ingredients into a large mixing bowl.
2. Stir well.
3. Using a tablespoon, cookie scoop, or ice cream scoop, roll dough into balls and place on a baking sheet.
4. Refrigerate for two hours and enjoy!

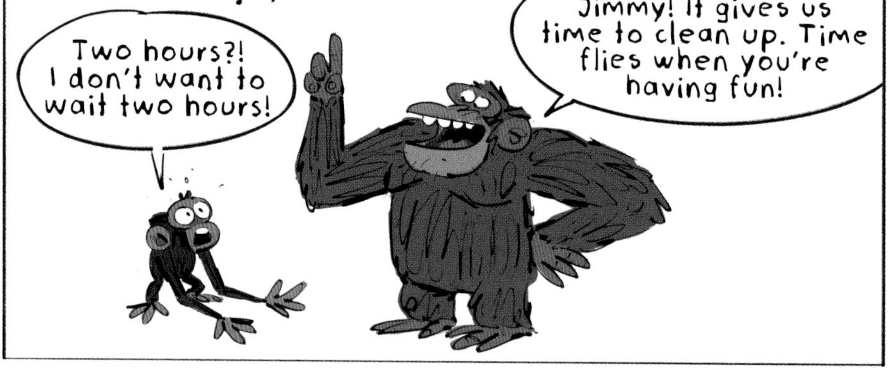
Two hours?! I don't want to wait two hours!
Don't worry, Jimmy! It gives us time to clean up. Time flies when you're having fun!

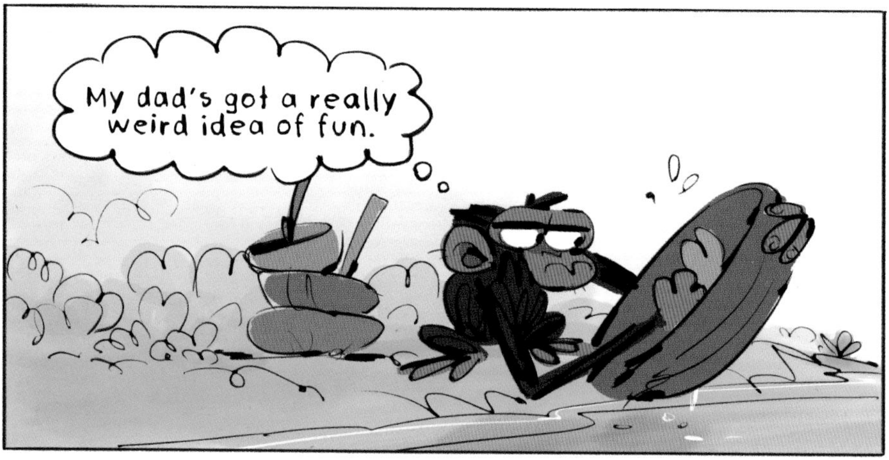
My dad's got a really weird idea of fun.

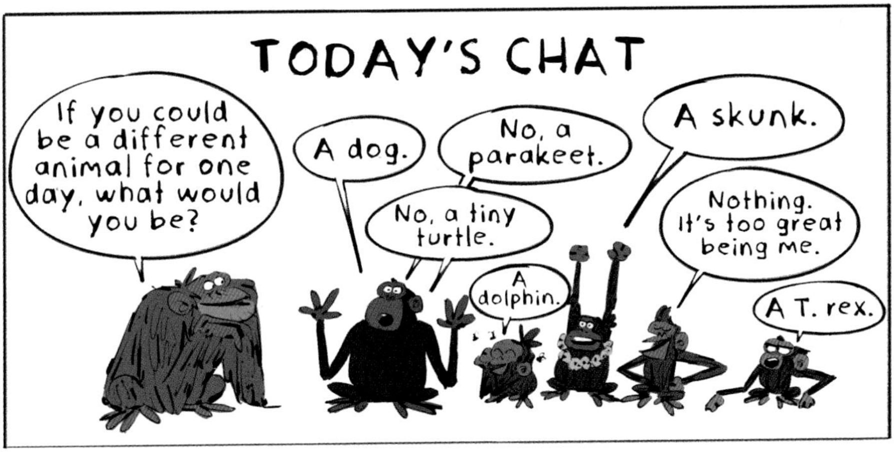
TODAY'S CHAT
If you could be a different animal for one day, what would you be?
A dog.
No, a parakeet.
No, a tiny turtle.
A dolphin.
A skunk.
Nothing. It's too great being me.
A T. rex.

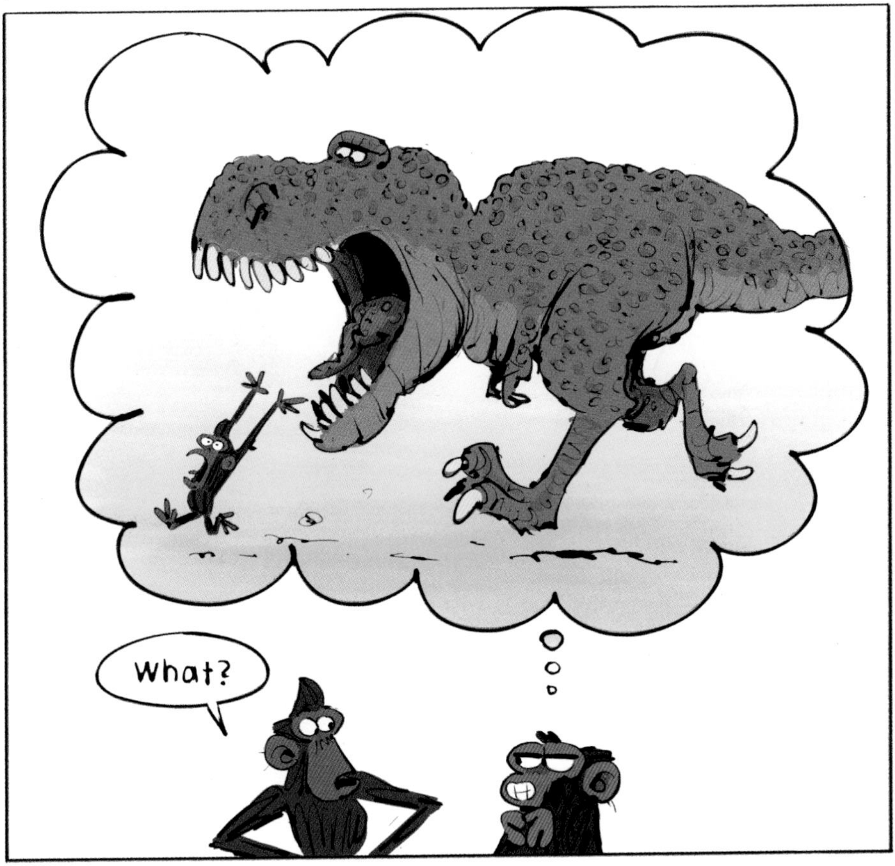
What?

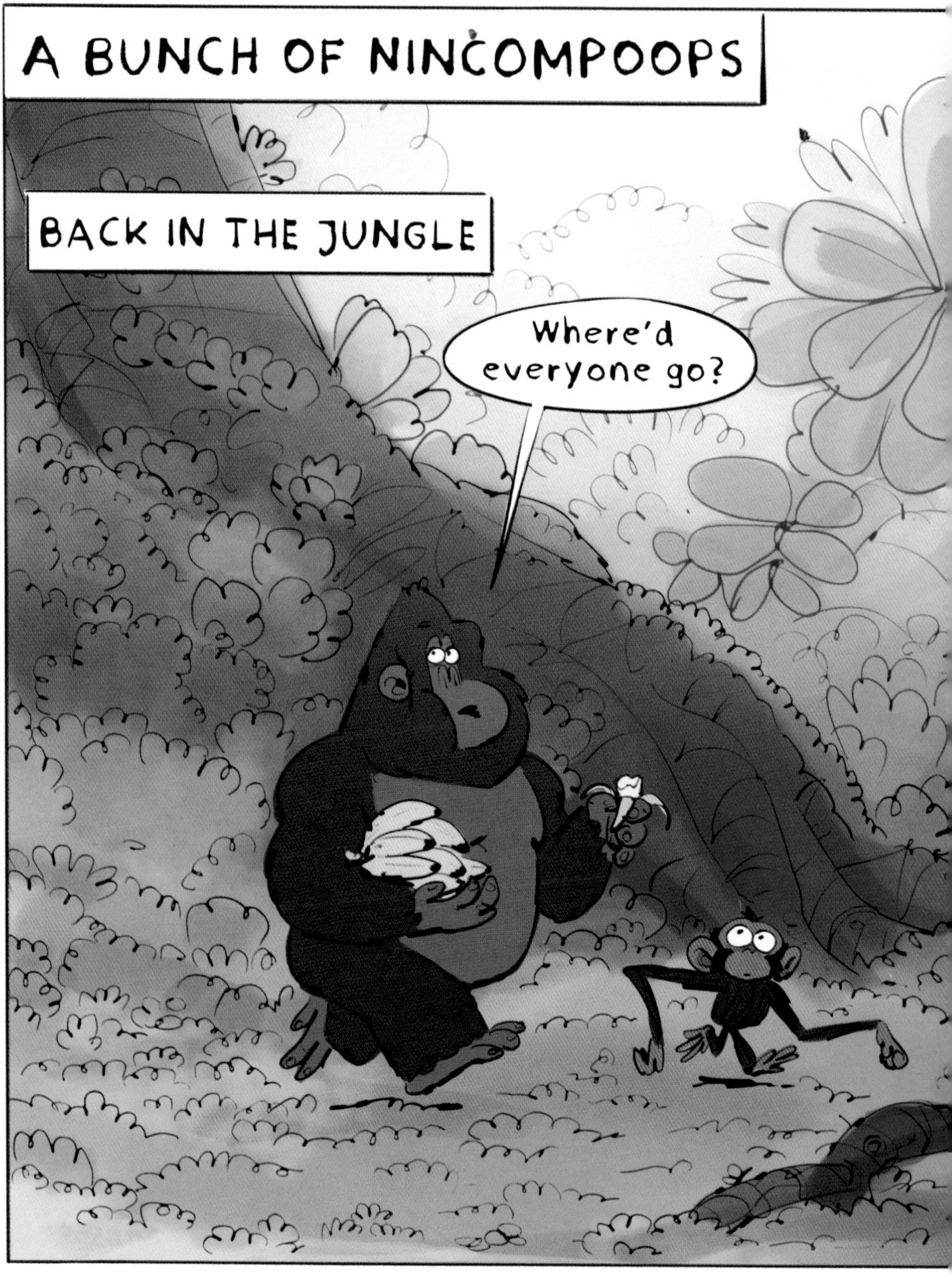
A BUNCH OF NINCOMPOOPS
BACK IN THE JUNGLE
Where'd everyone go?

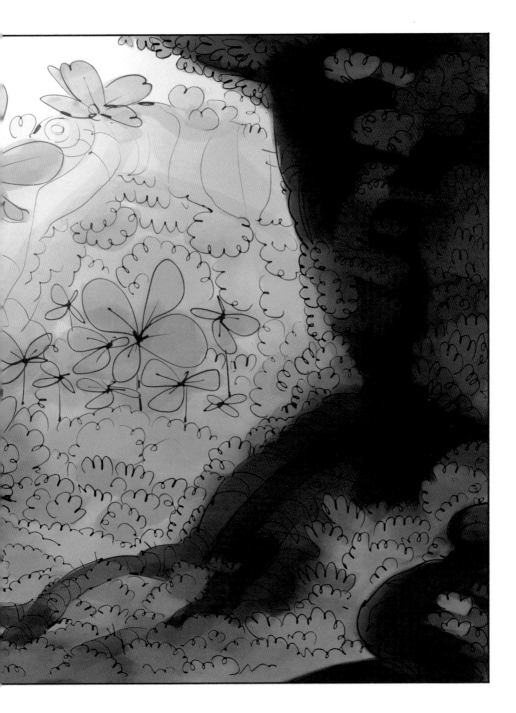

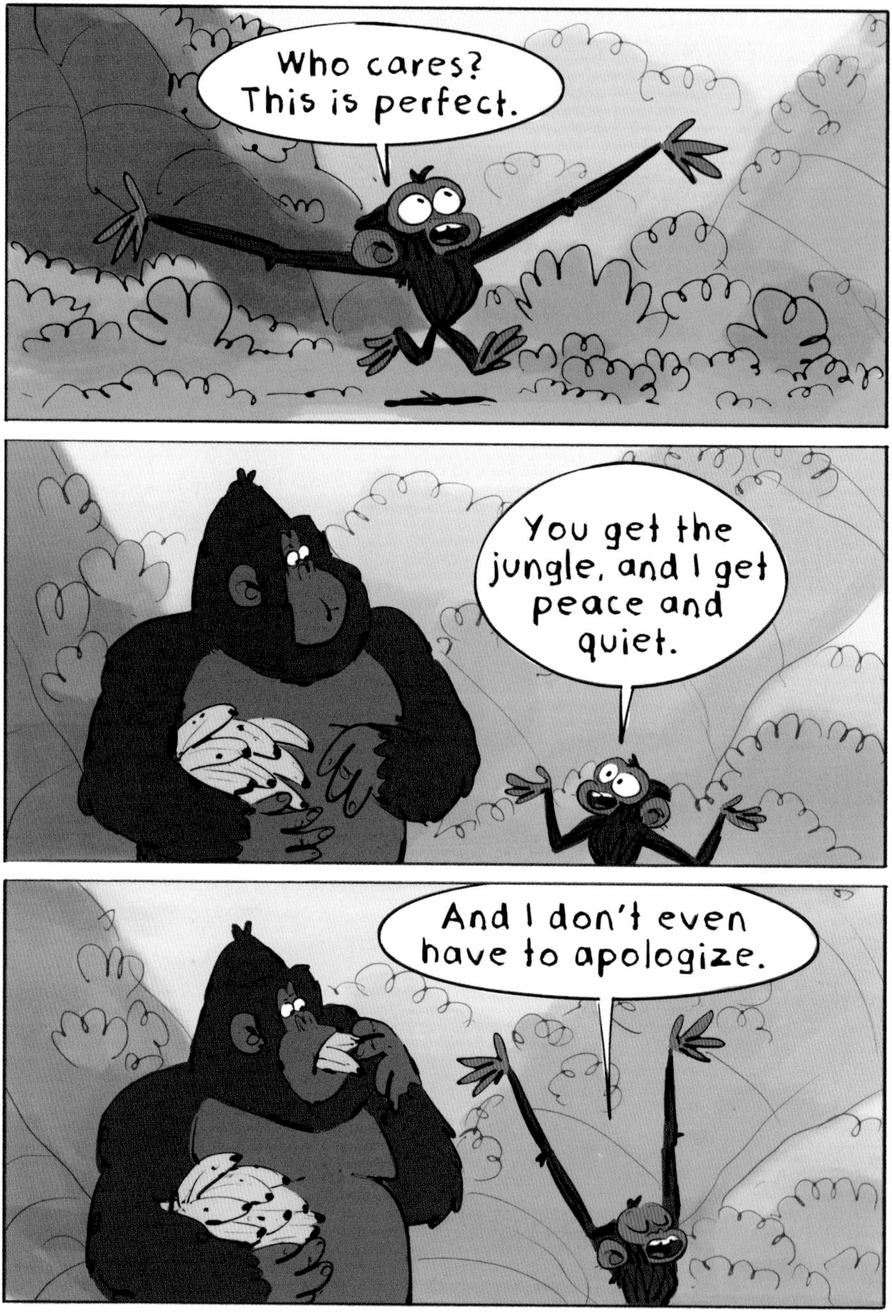
Who cares? This is perfect.
You get the jungle, and I get peace and quiet.
And I don't even have to apologize.

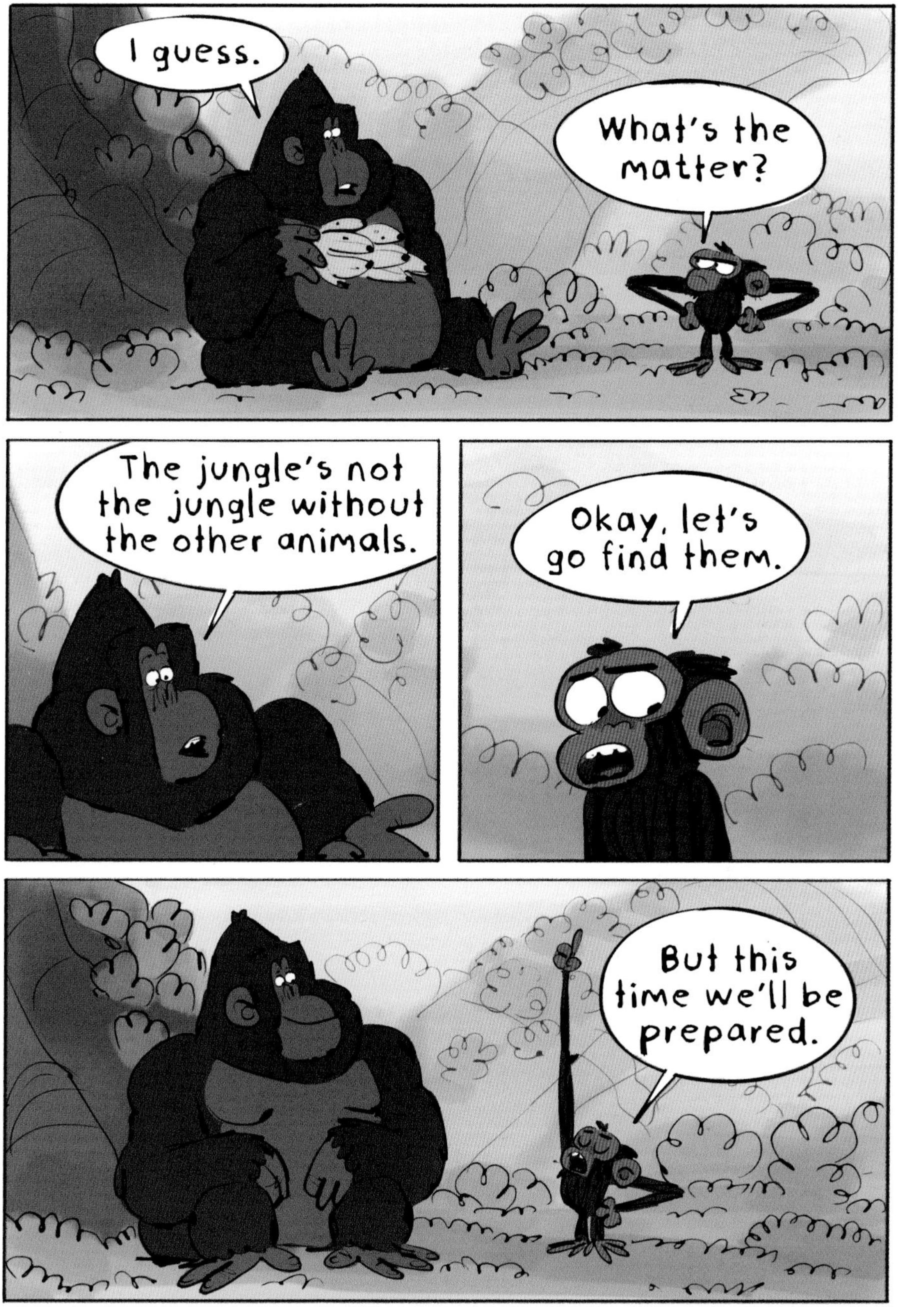
I guess.
What's the matter?
The jungle's not the jungle without the other animals.
Okay, let's go find them.
But this time we'll be prepared.

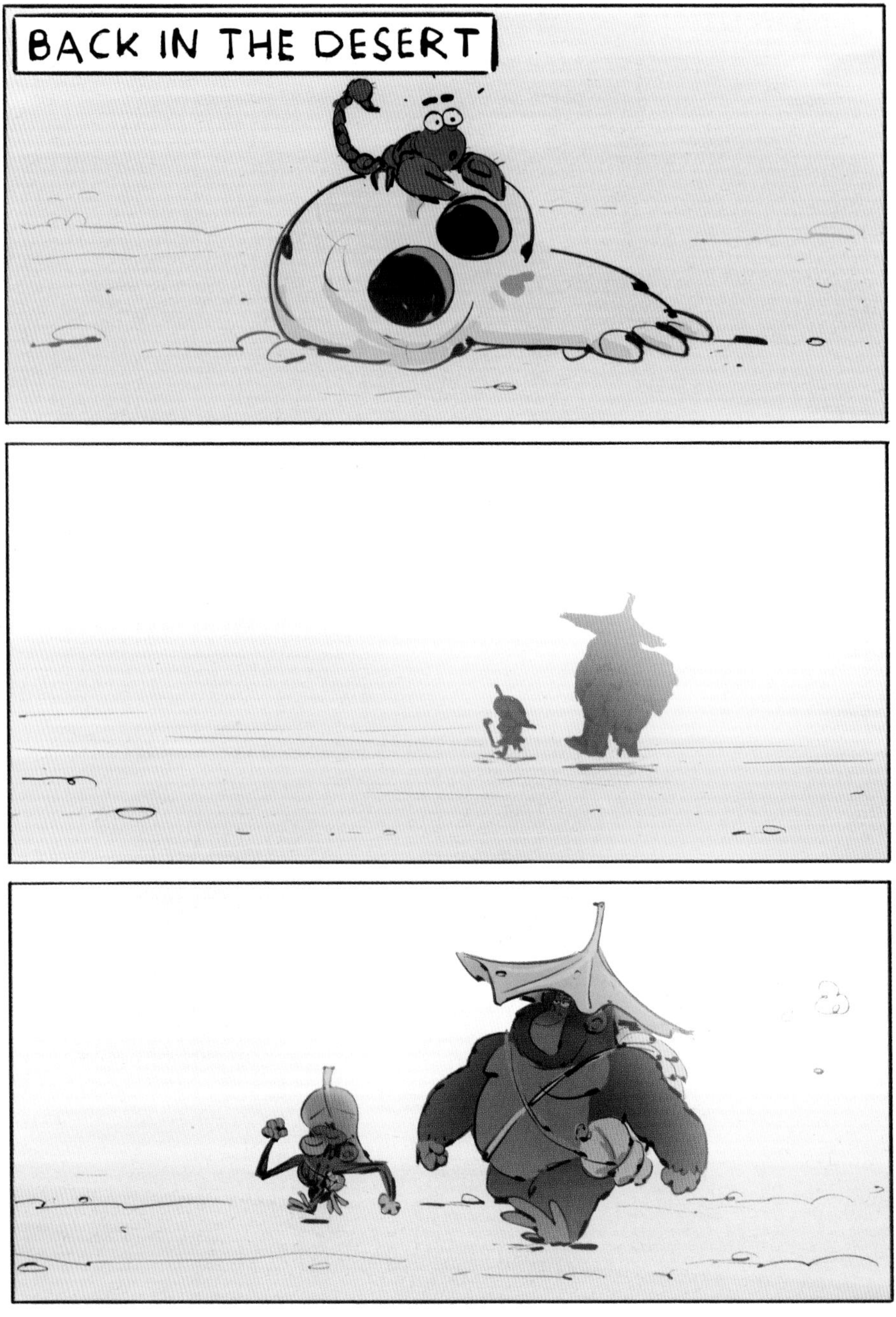
BACK IN THE DESERT

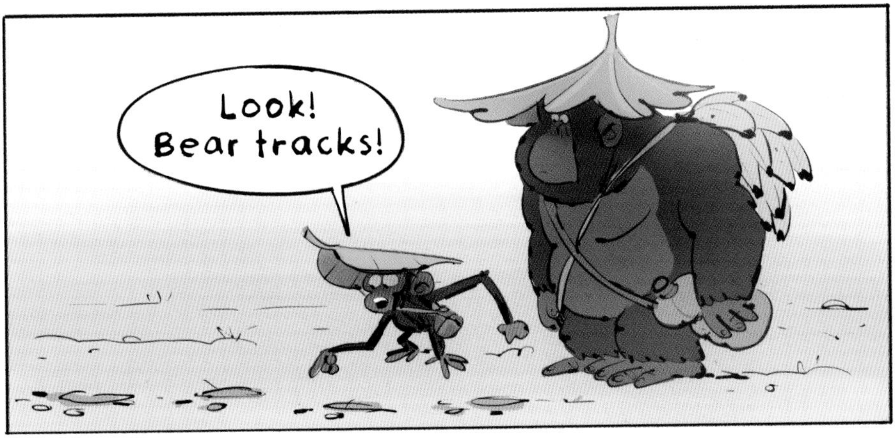
Look! Bear tracks!

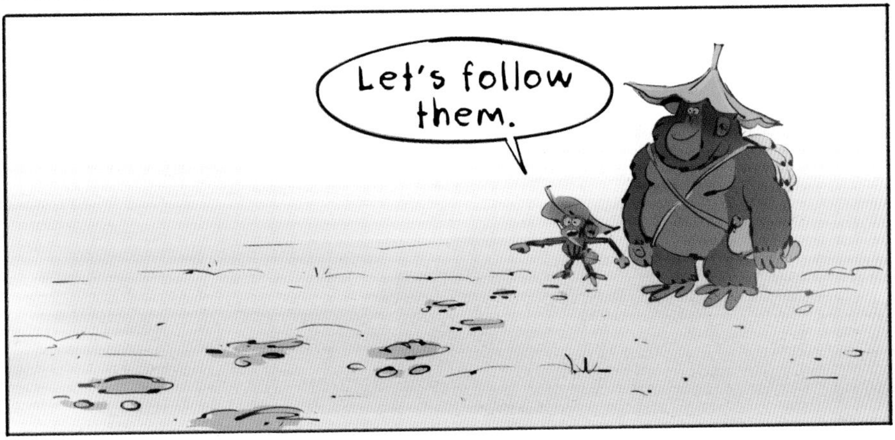
Let's follow them.

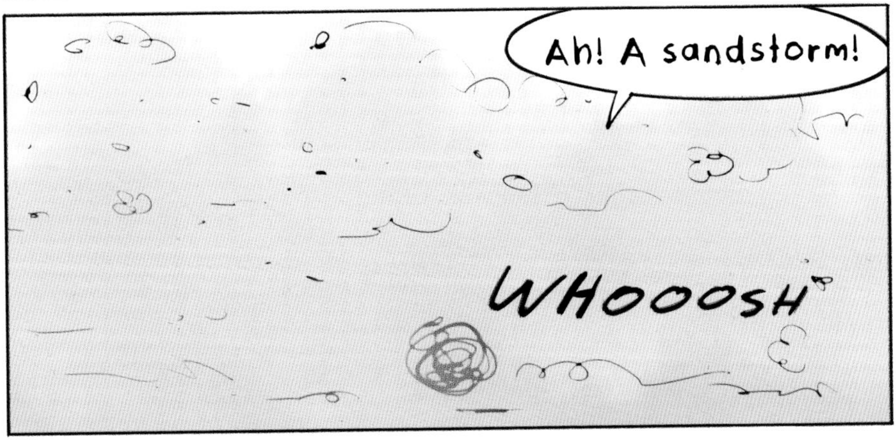
Ah! A sandstorm!
WHOOOSH

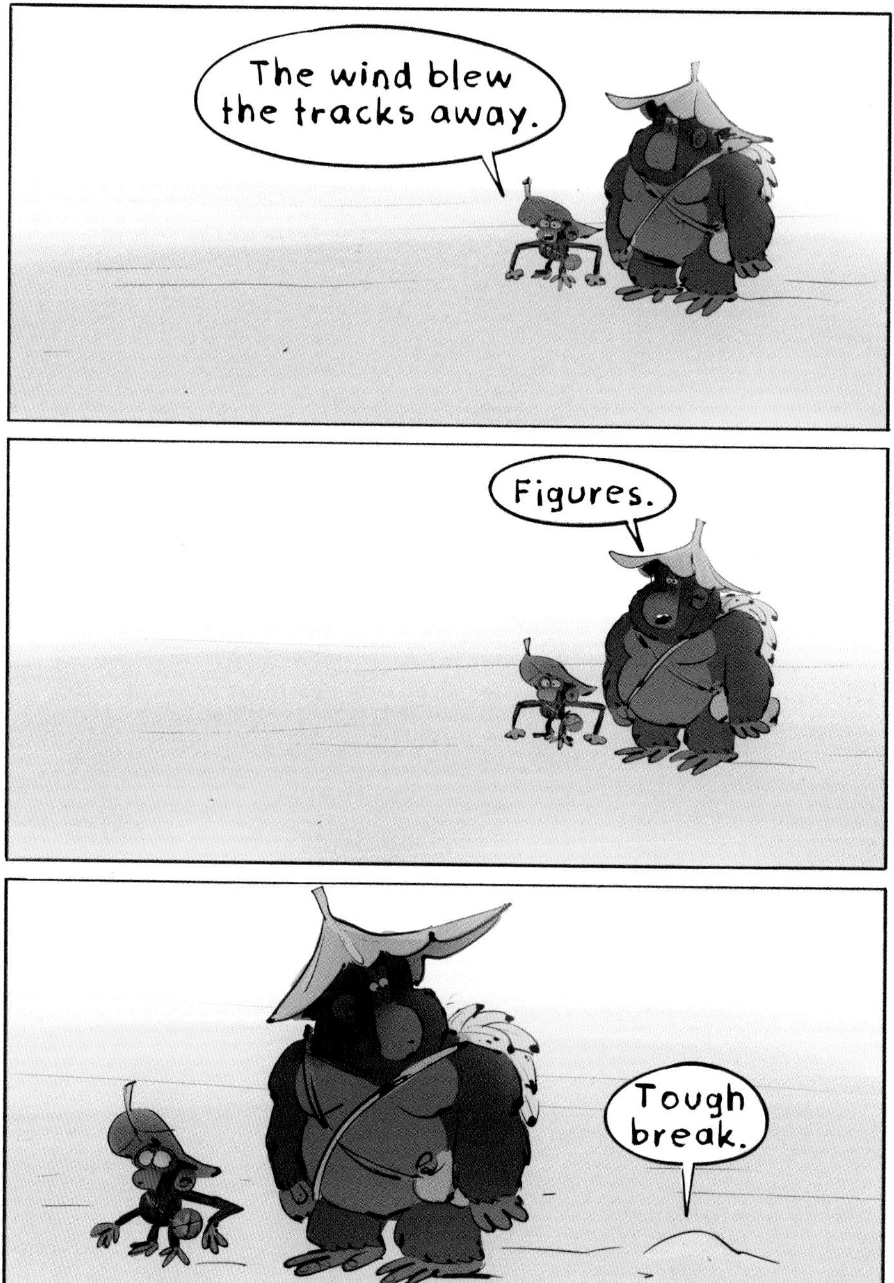
The wind blew the tracks away.
Figures.
Tough break.

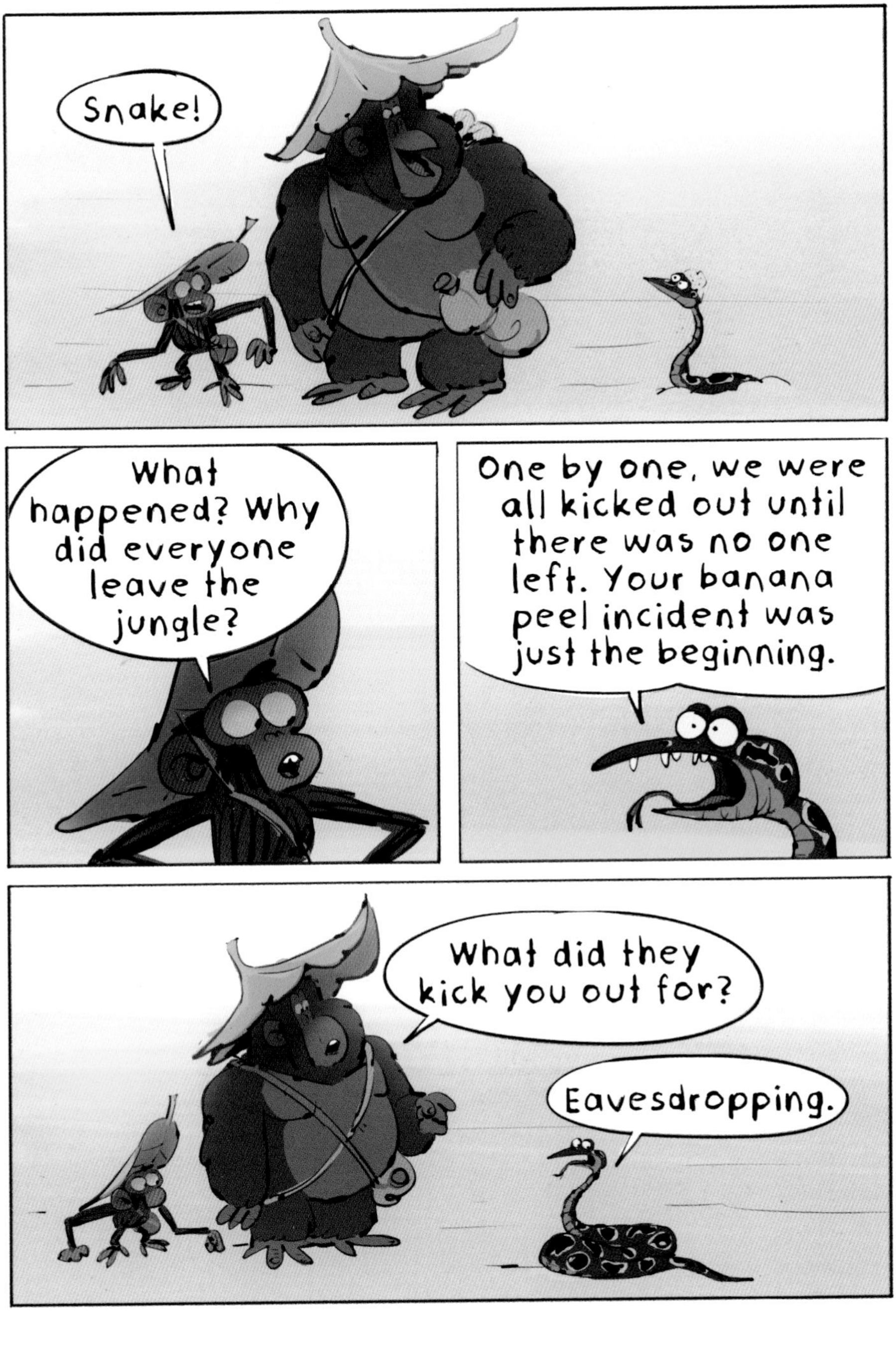

Snake!
What happened? Why did everyone leave the jungle?
One by one, we were all kicked out until there was no one left. Your banana peel incident was just the beginning.
What did they kick you out for?
Eavesdropping.

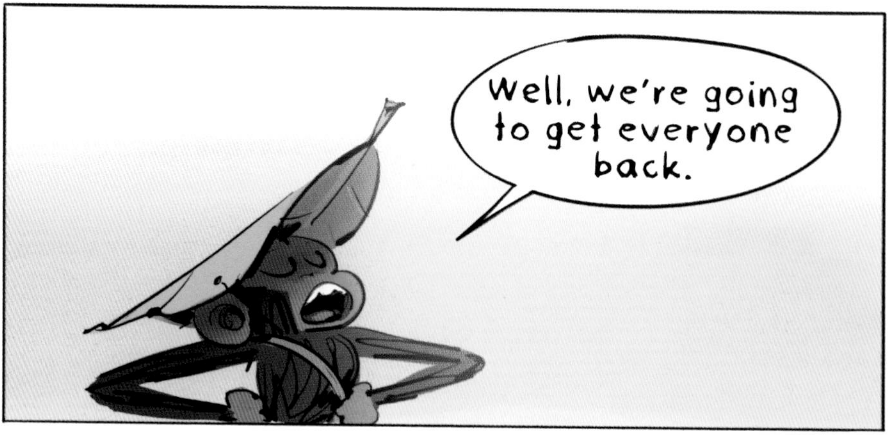
Well, we're going to get everyone back.

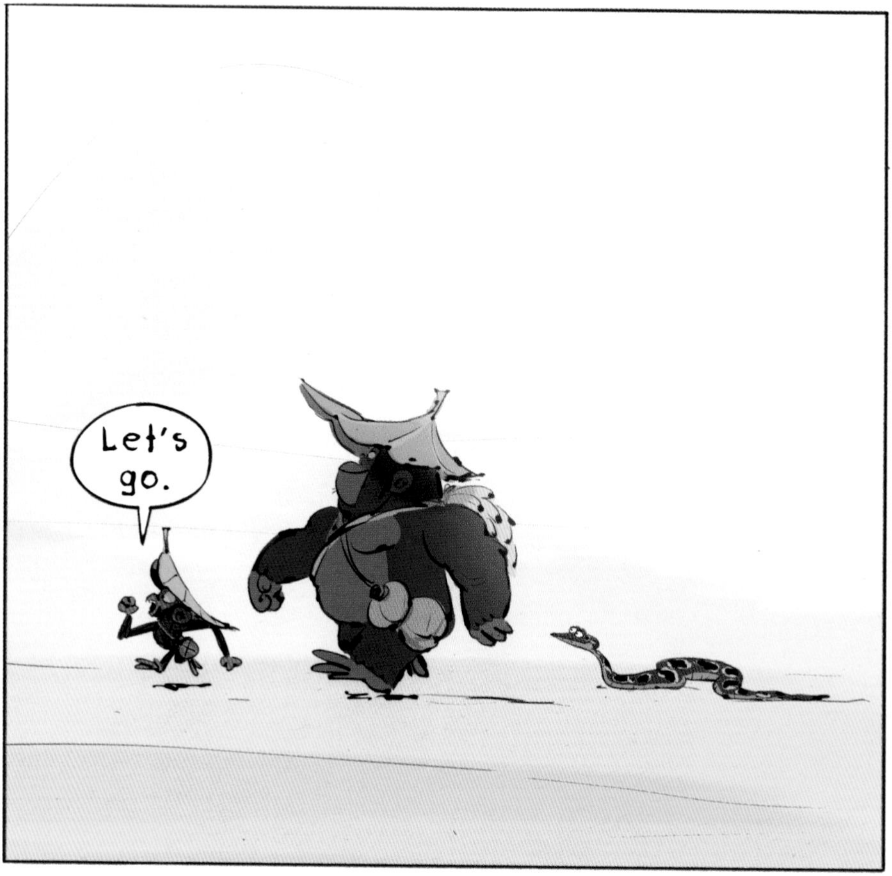
Let's go.

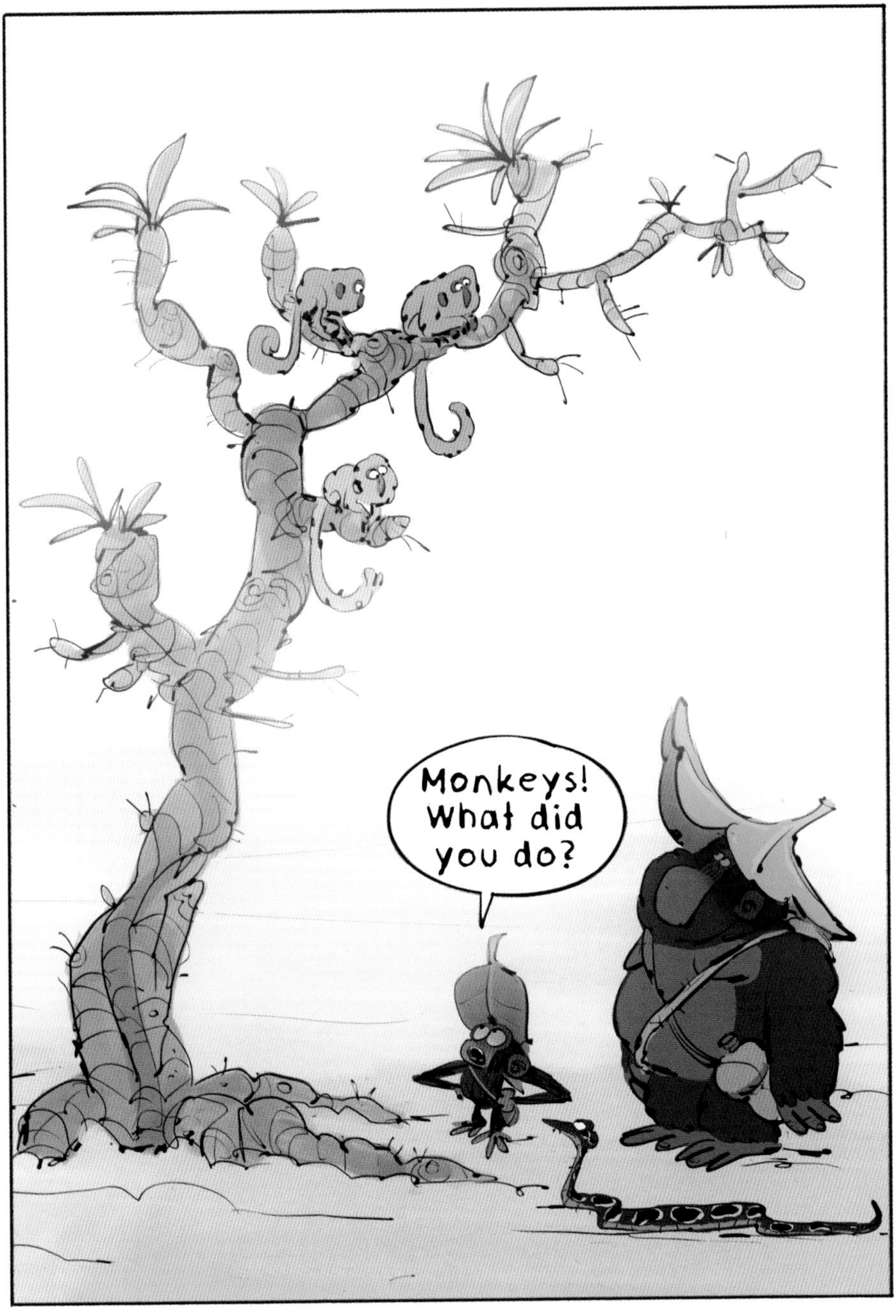
Monkeys! What did you do?

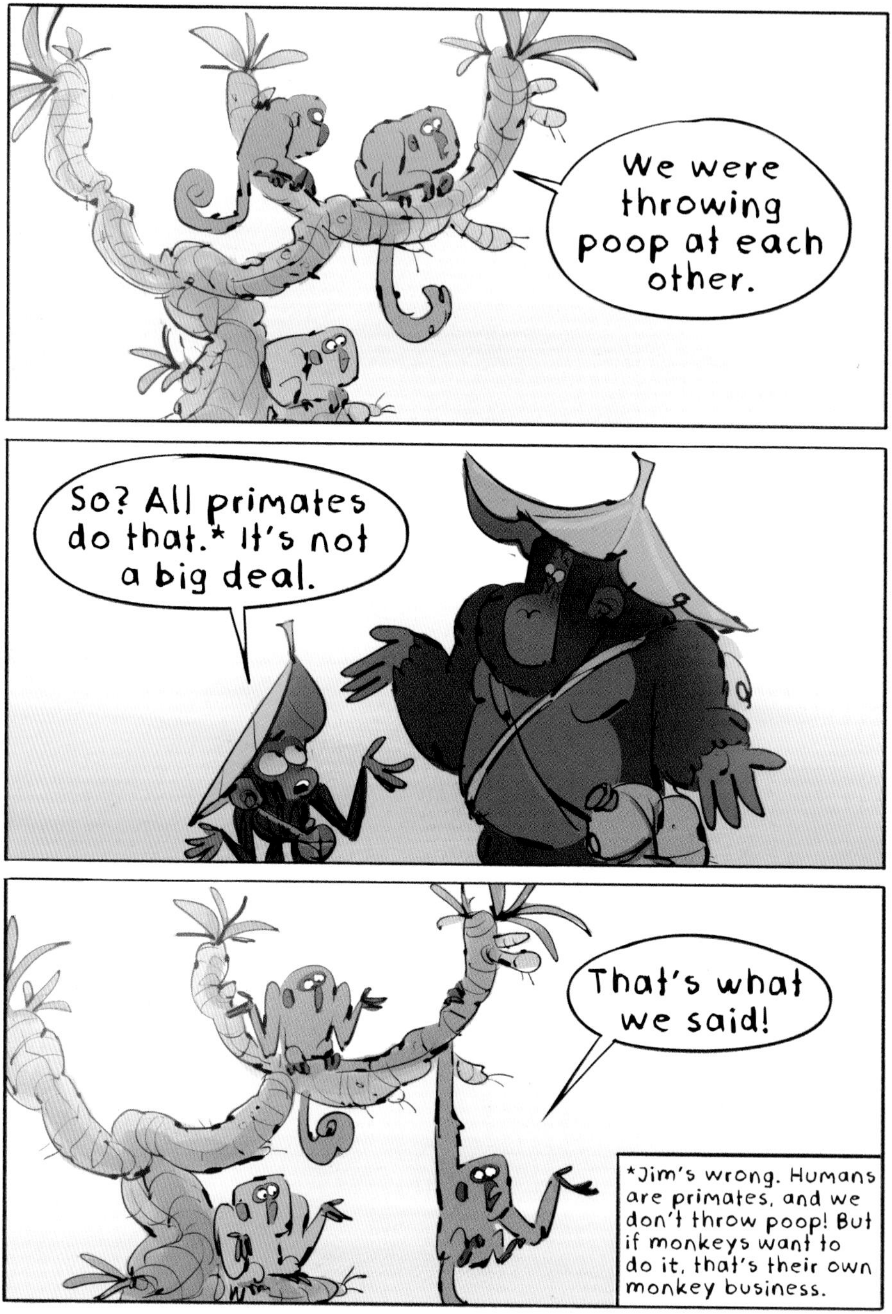
We were throwing poop at each other.
So? All primates do that.* It's not a big deal.
That's what we said!
*Jim's wrong. Humans are primates, and we don't throw poop! But if monkeys want to do it, that's their own monkey business.

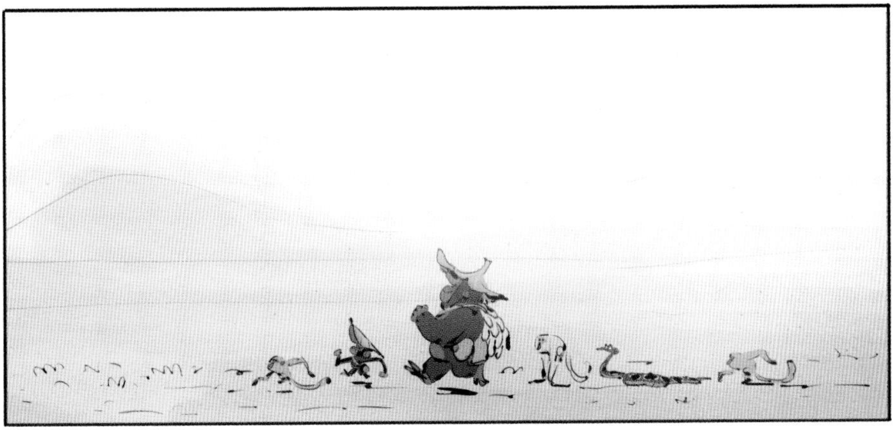

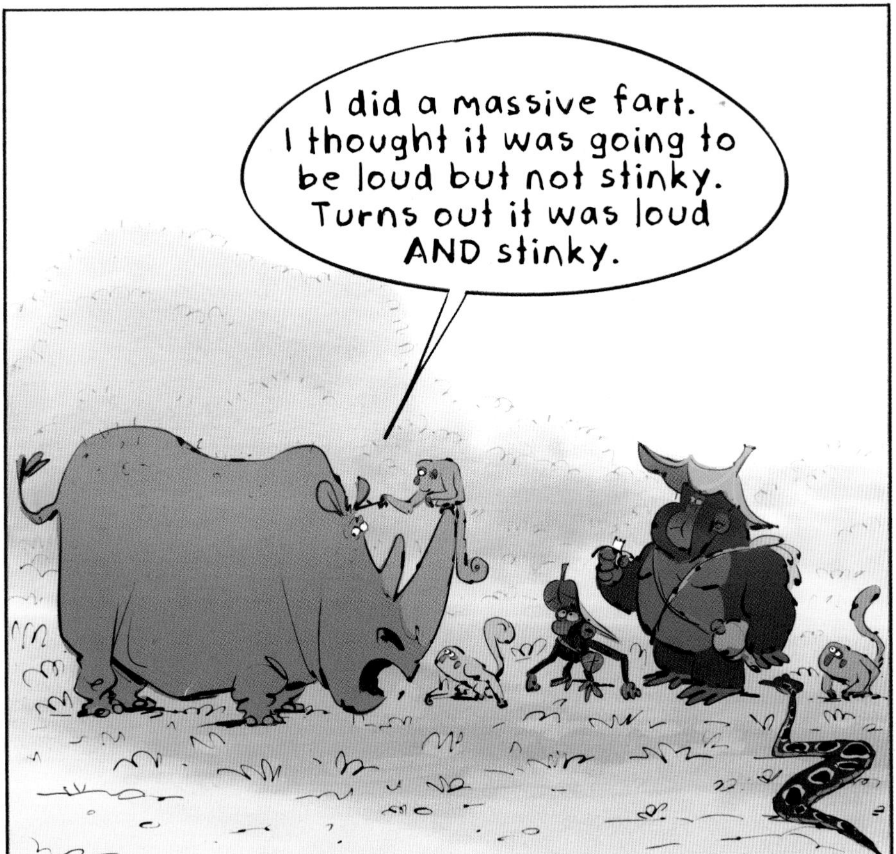
I did a massive fart. I thought it was going to be loud but not stinky. Turns out it was loud AND stinky.

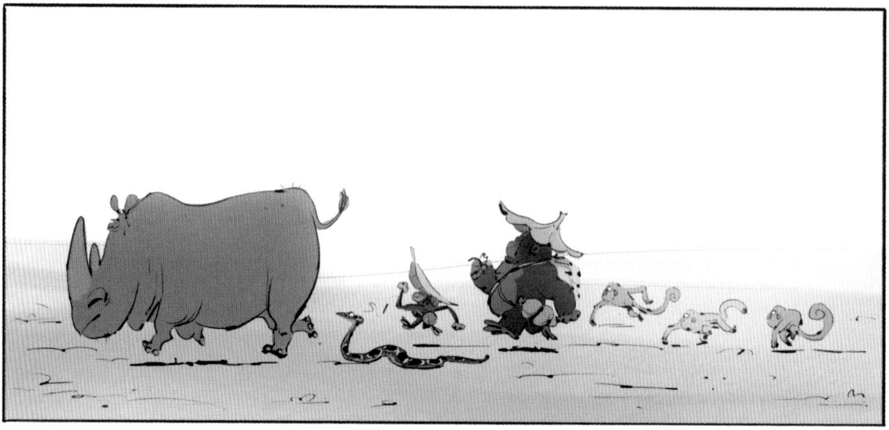

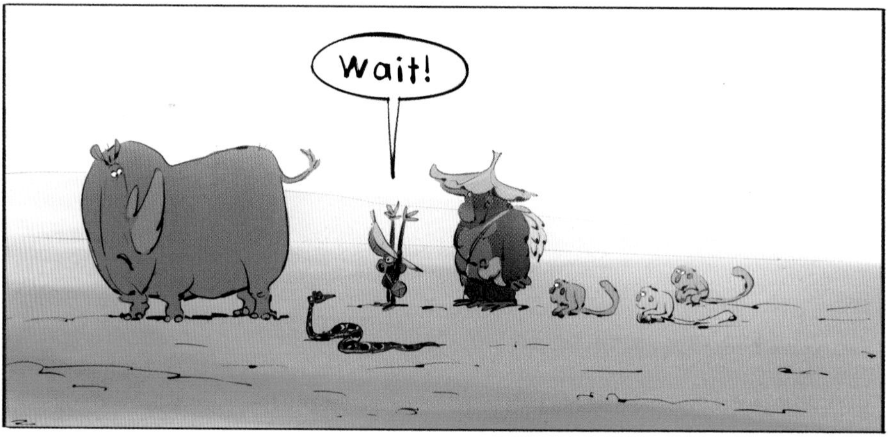
Wait!

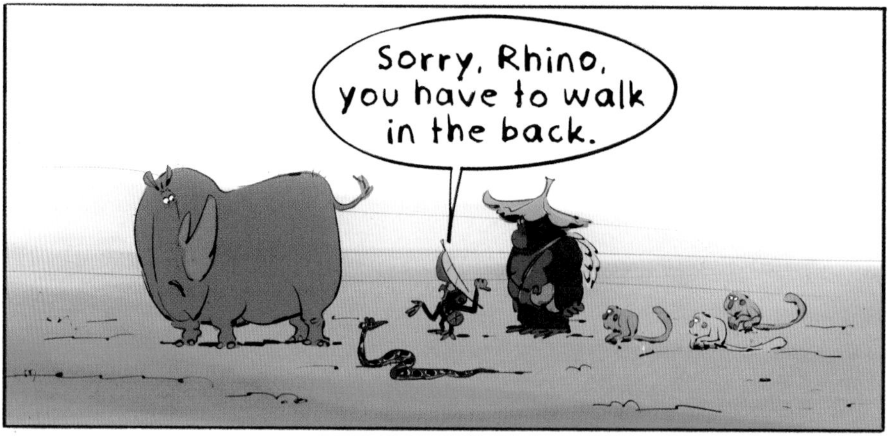
Sorry, Rhino, you have to walk in the back.

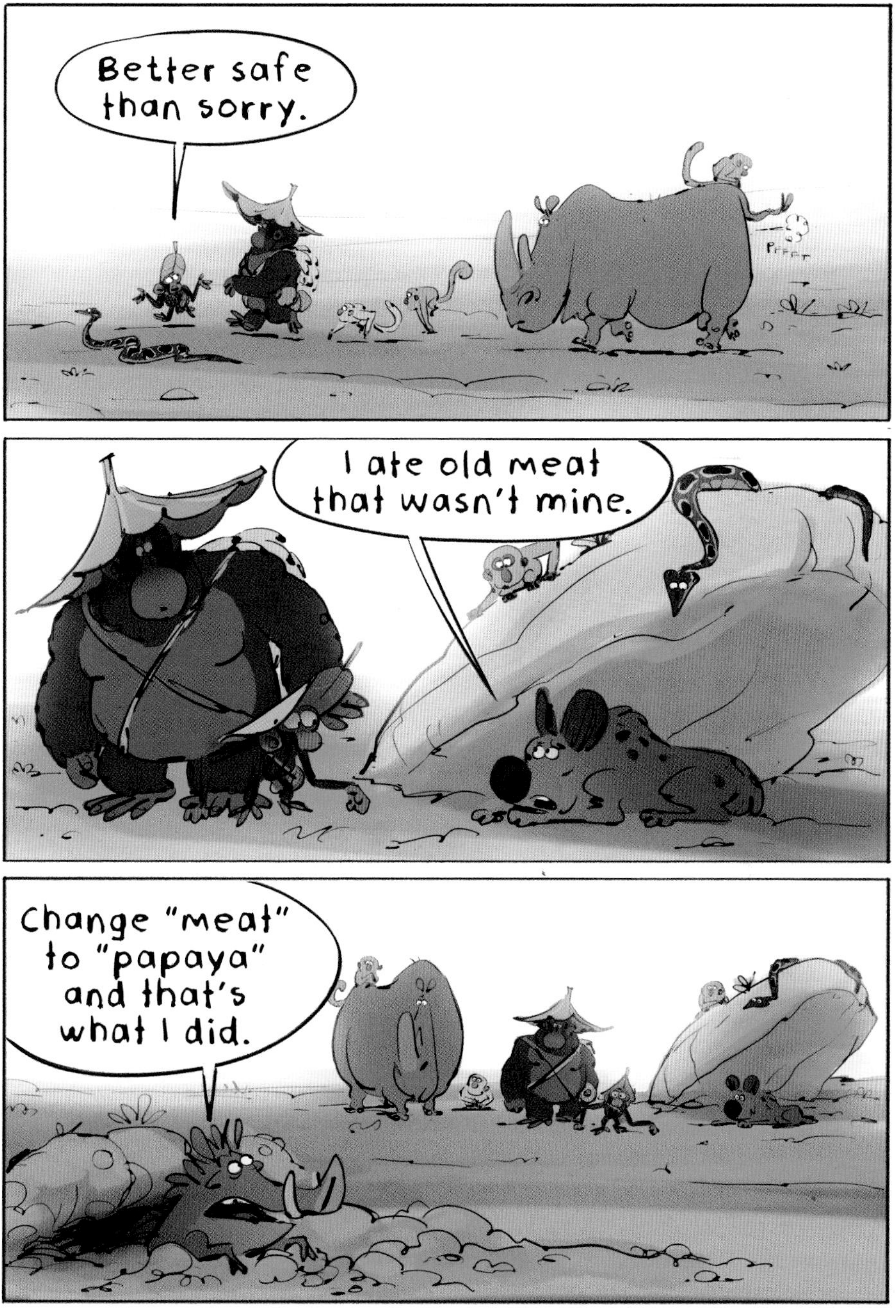
Better safe than sorry.
PFFFT
I ate old meat that wasn't mine.
Change "meat" to "papaya" and that's what I did.

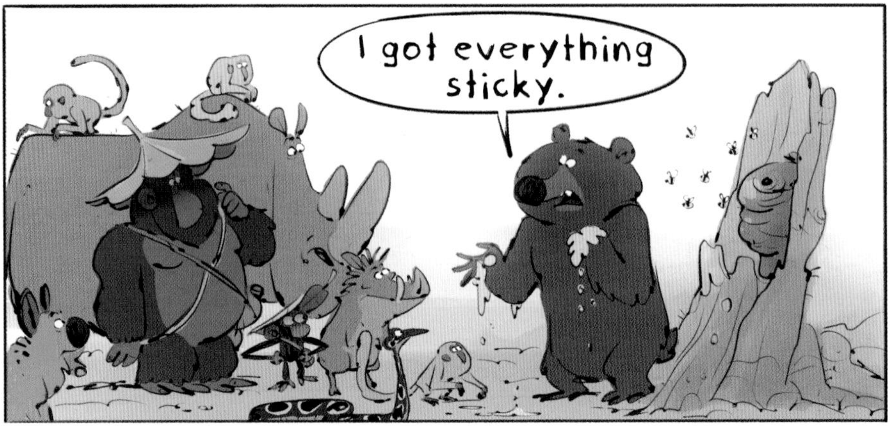
I got everything sticky.

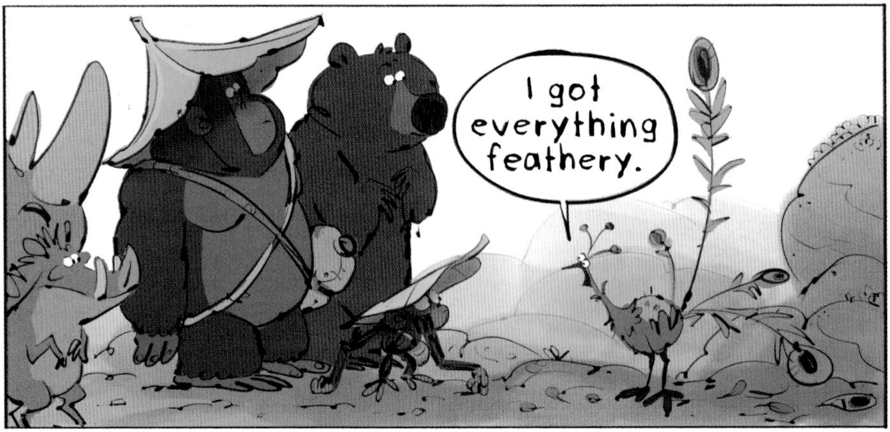
I got everything feathery.

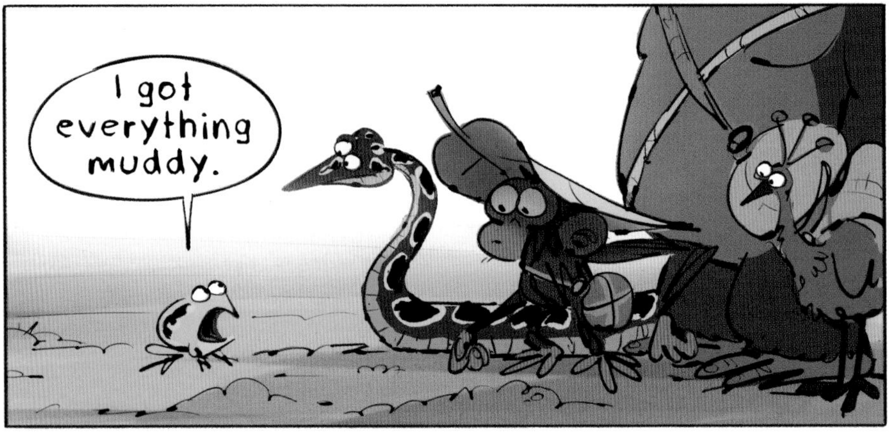
I got everything muddy.

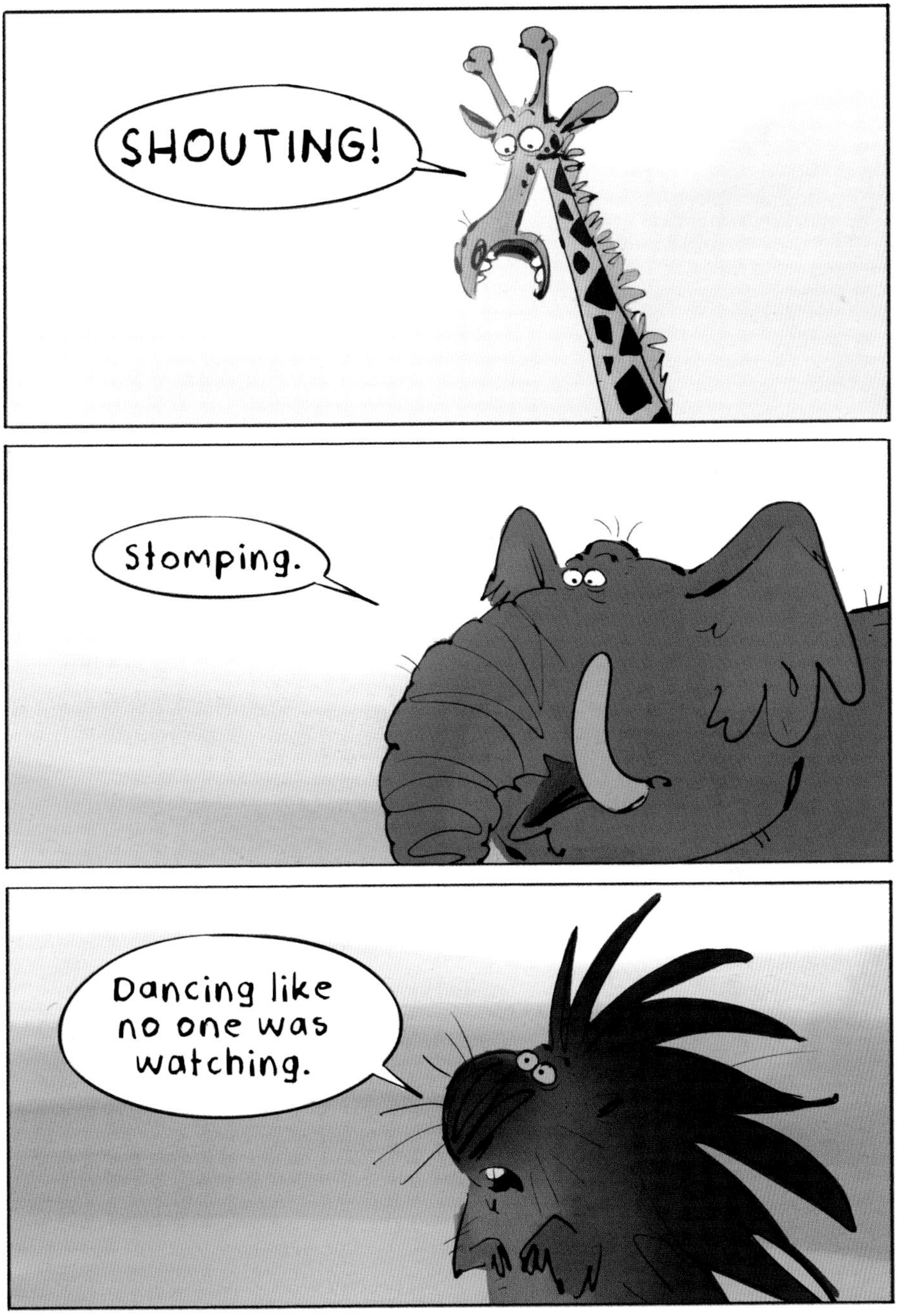
SHOUTING!
Stomping.
Dancing like no one was watching.

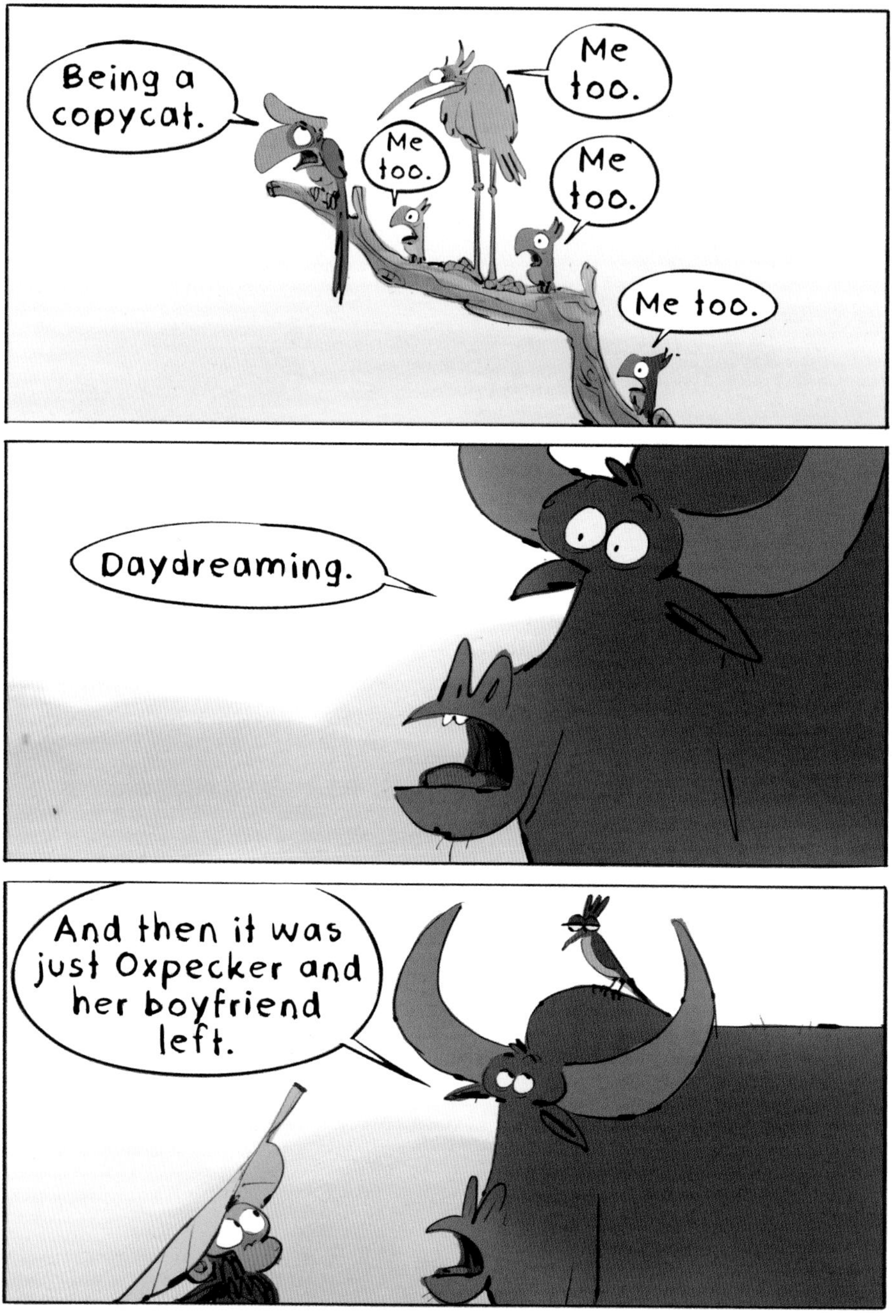
Being a copycat.
Me too.
Me too.
Me too.
Me too.
Daydreaming.
And then it was just Oxpecker and her boyfriend left.

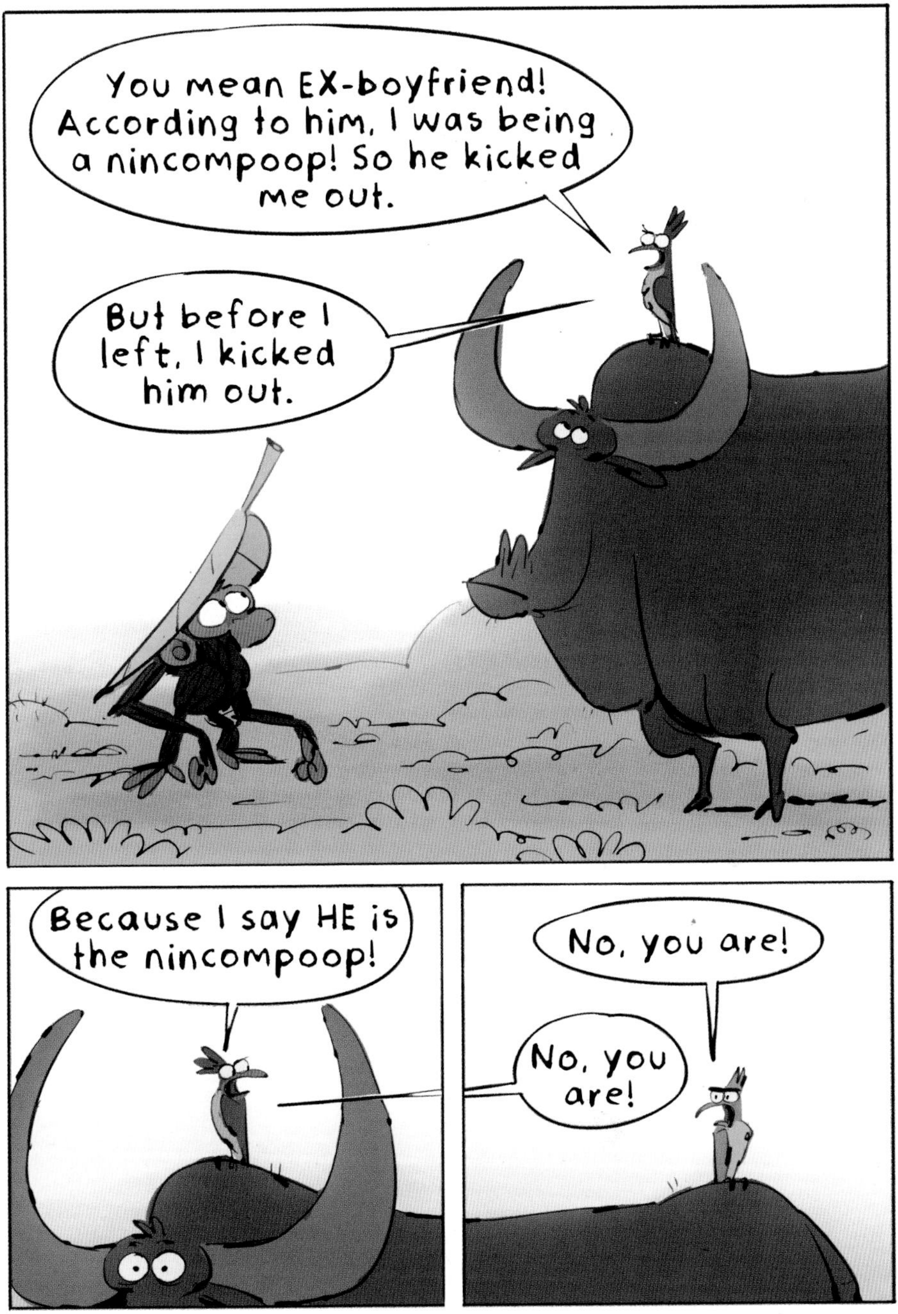
You mean EX-boyfriend! According to him, I was being a nincompoop! So he kicked me out.
But before I left, I kicked him out.
Because I say HE is the nincompoop!
No, you are!
No, you are!

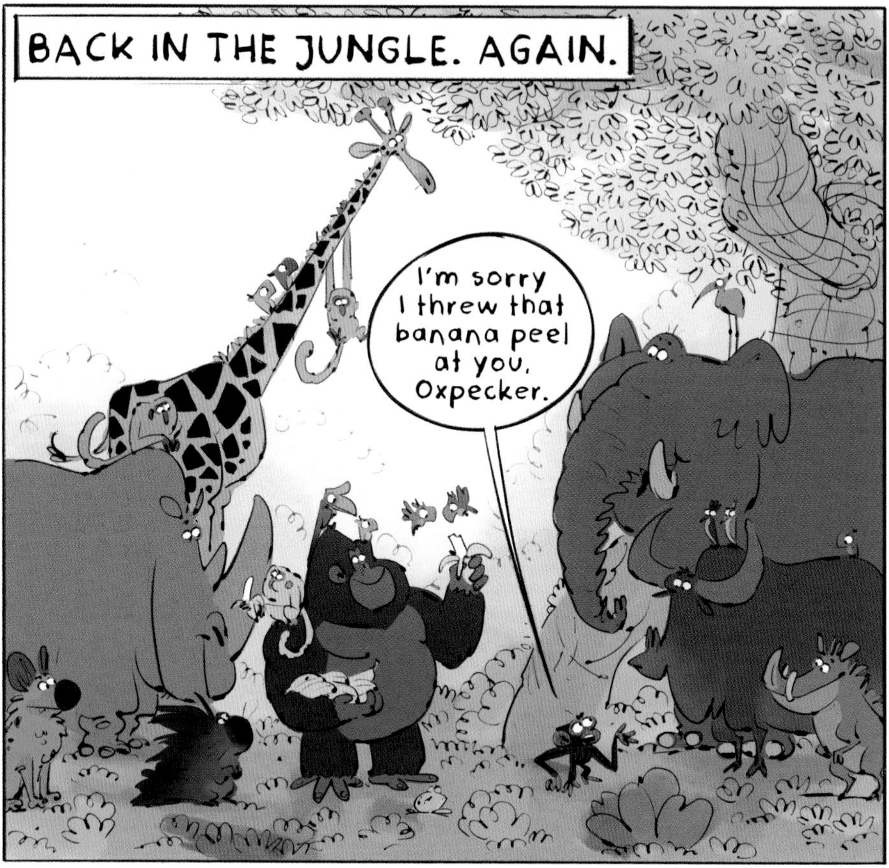
BACK IN THE JUNGLE. AGAIN.
I'm sorry I threw that banana peel at you, Oxpecker.

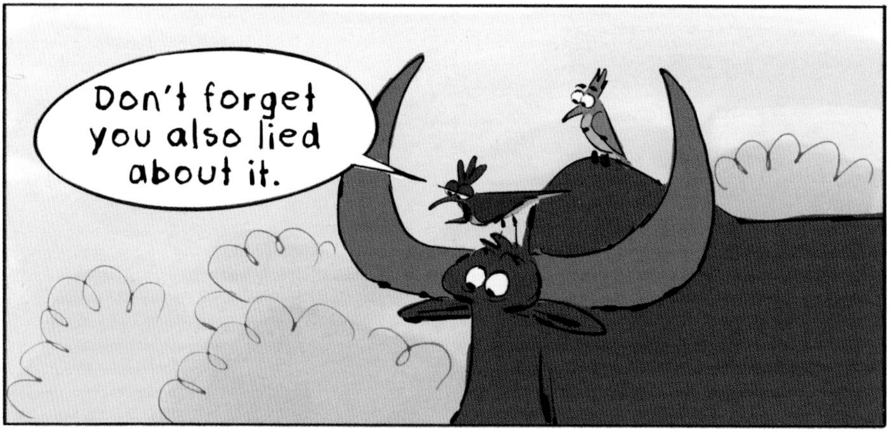
Don't forget you also lied about it.

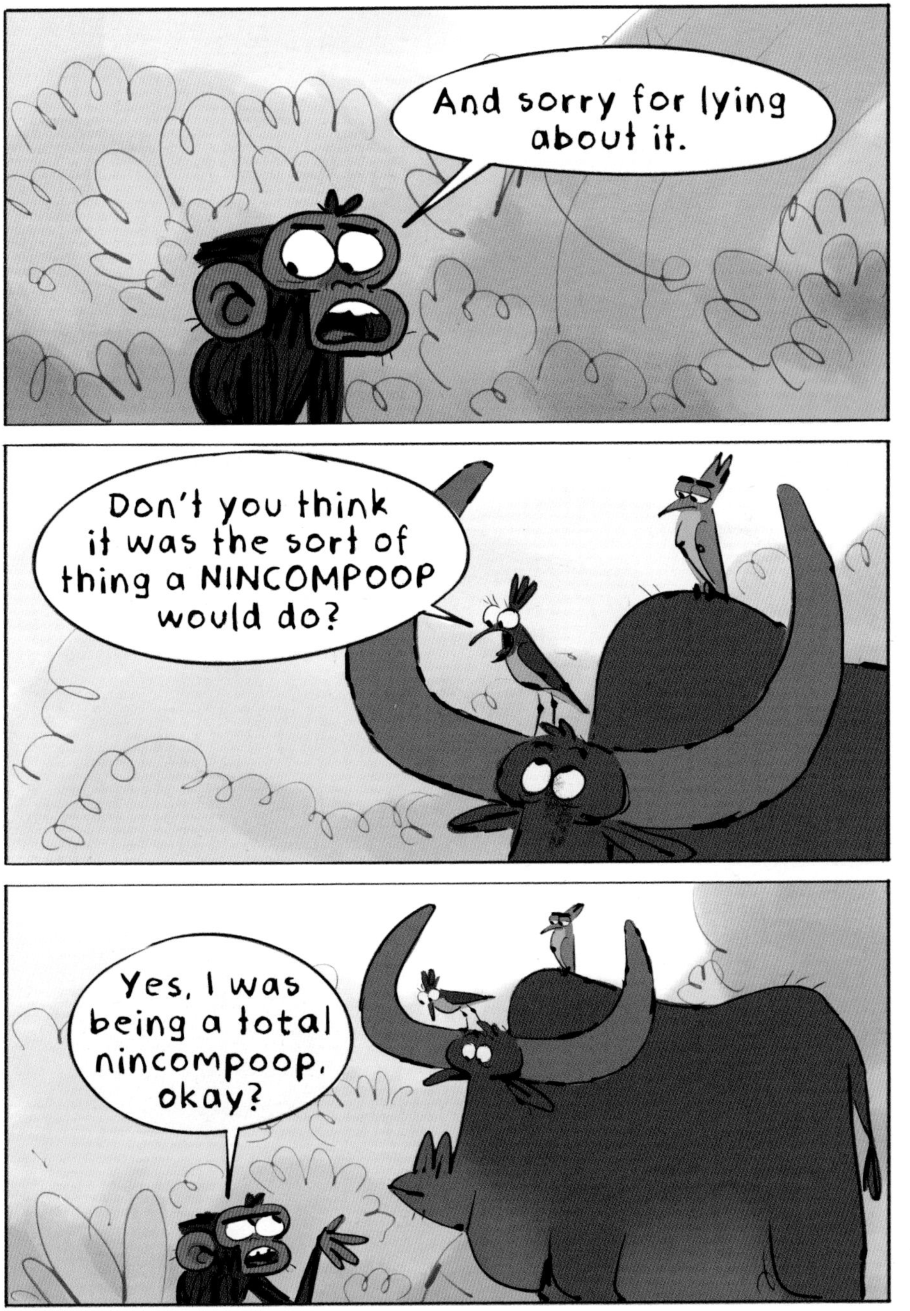
And sorry for lying about it.
Don't you think it was the sort of thing a NINCOMPOOP would do?
Yes, I was being a total nincompoop, okay?

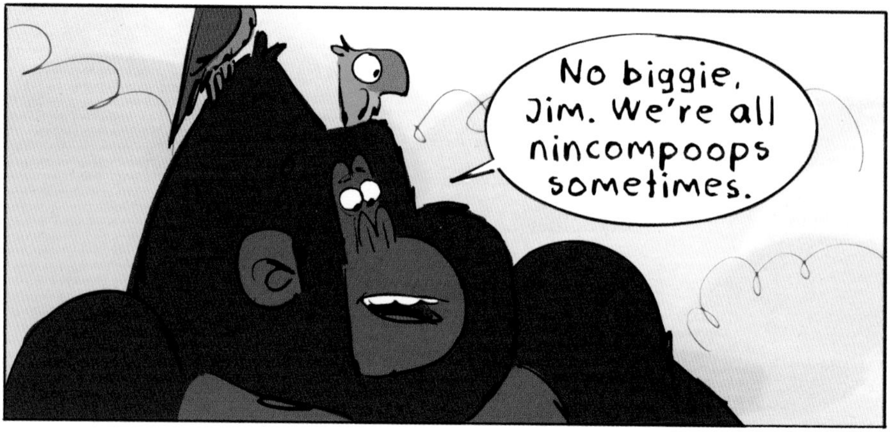
No biggie, Jim. We're all nincompoops sometimes.

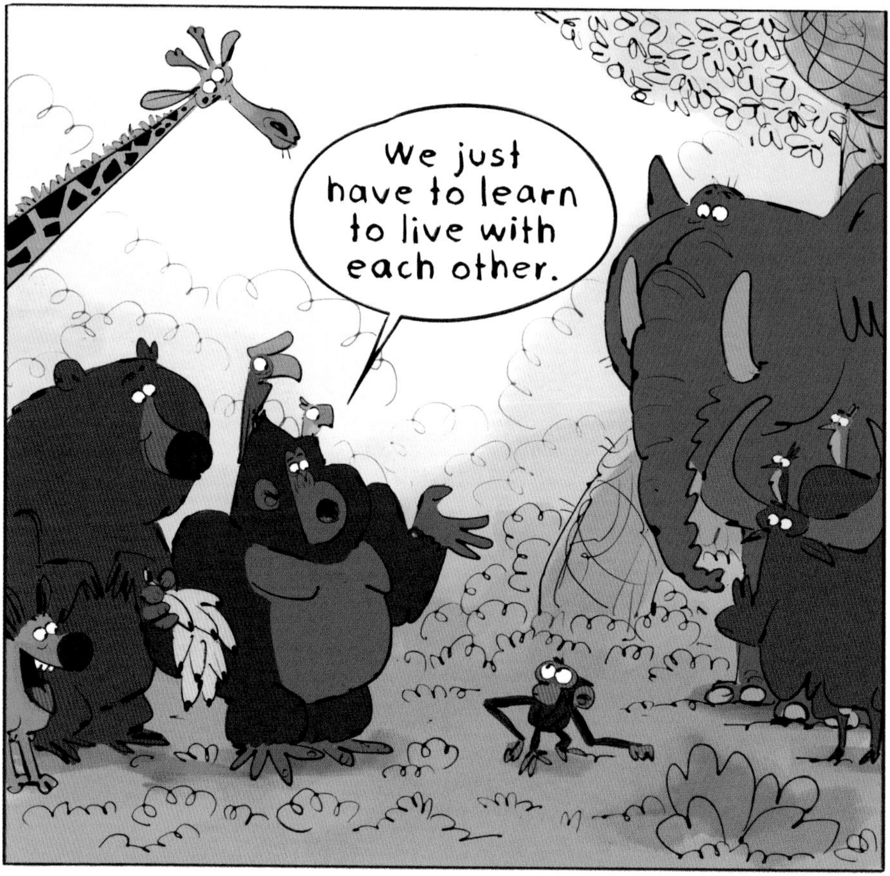
We just have to learn to live with each other.

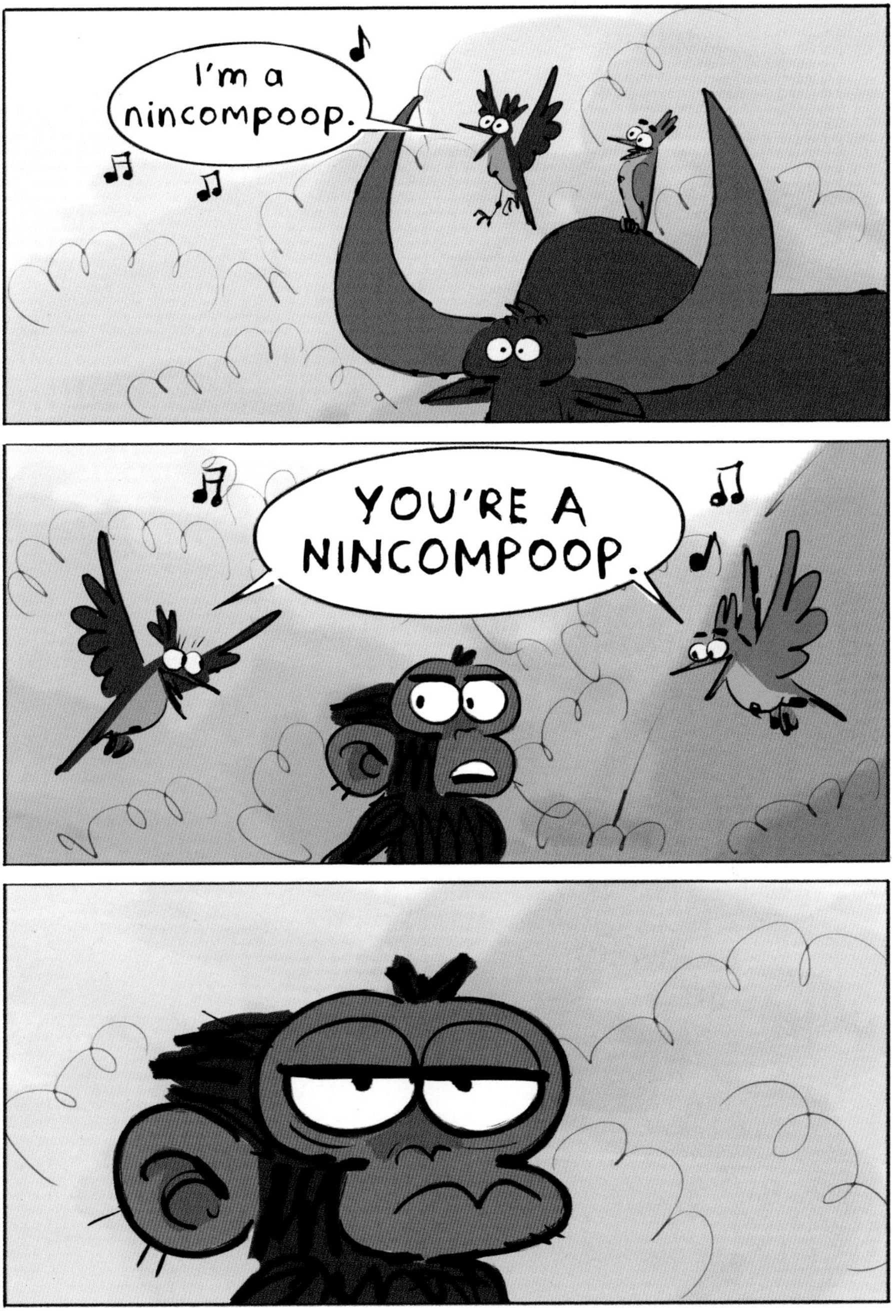
I'm a nincompoop.
YOU'RE A NINCOMPOOP.

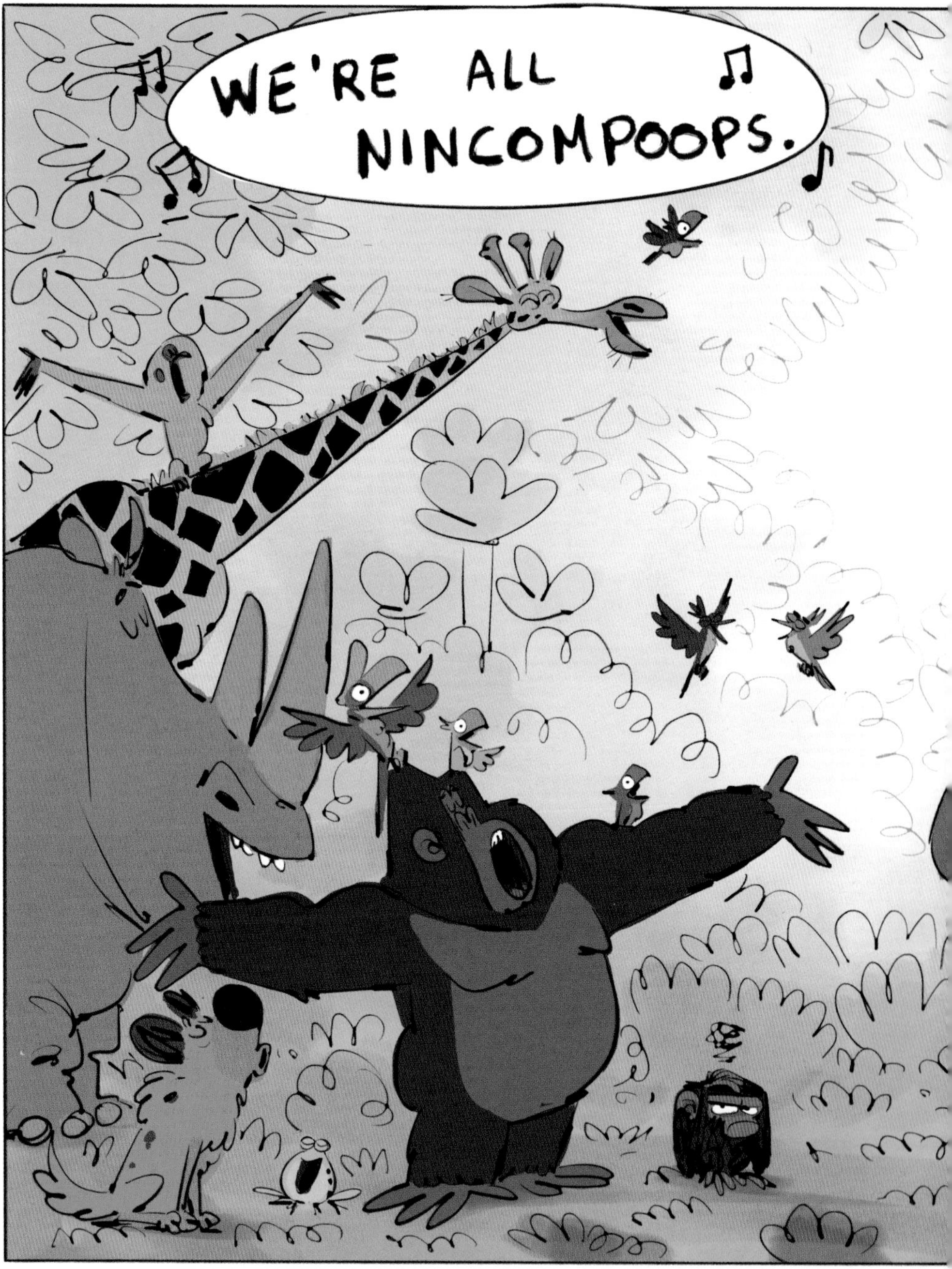
WE'RE ALL NINCOMPOOPS.

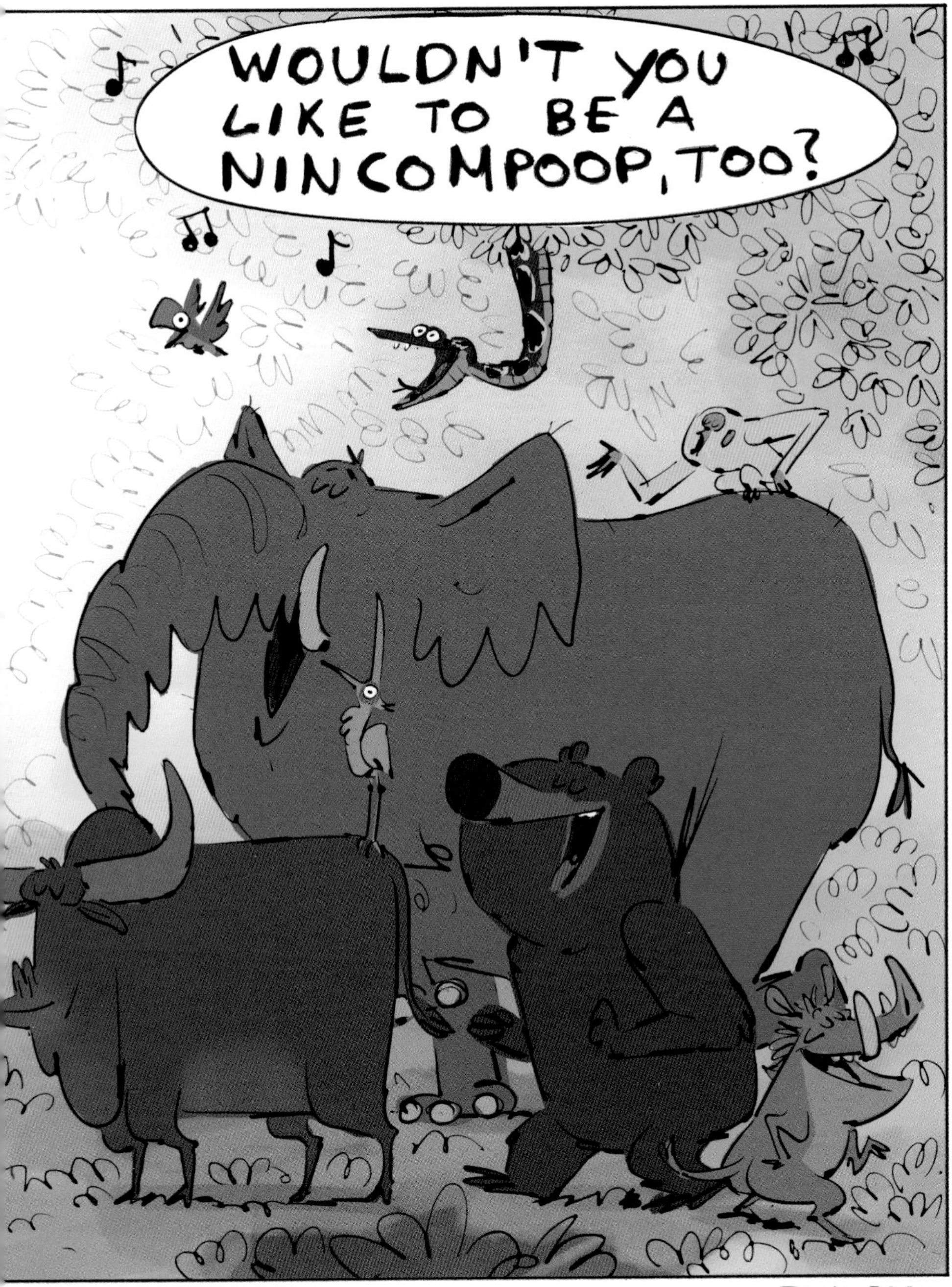
WOULDN'T YOU LIKE TO BE A NINCOMPOOP, TOO?

THE END

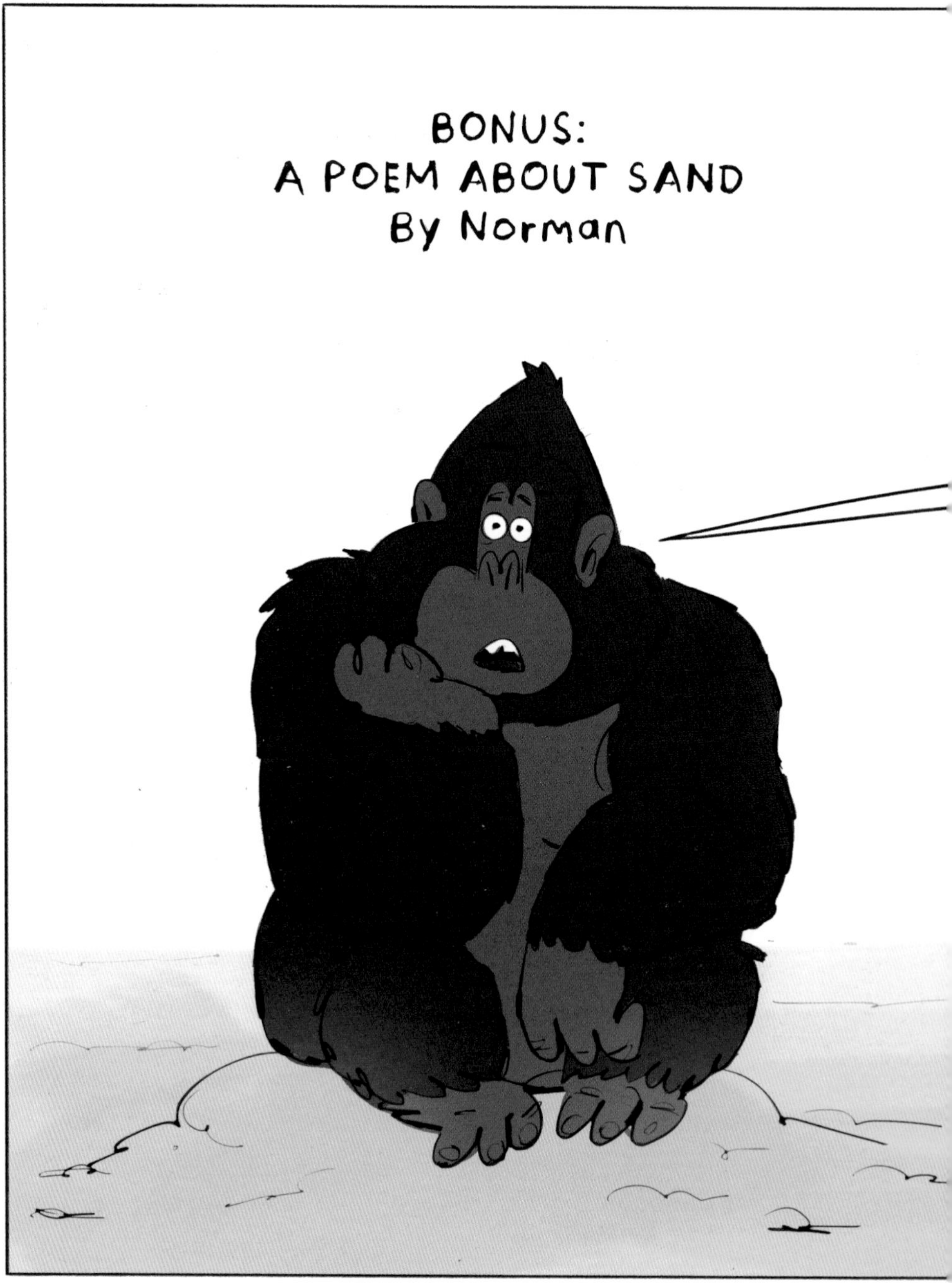
BONUS:
A POEM ABOUT SAND
By Norman